a Pure Slush book

praise for *The Company of Men*

With the clarity of the child's eye and the wisdom of the adult's hindsight seamlessly working together in the writer's voice, Brenta effortlessly reels the reader into her charming fictional memoir. While all the family members — as well as the servants who tend them — are deftly drawn, the conservative and indomitable grandmother is the pivotal character. Her slow but astonishing transformation teaches the young girl timeless lessons about class and power and love. If you know and adore Italy even a little bit, you will fall under the languid and colorful spell of *The Company of Men*. Bellissimo.

Laurie Taylor, author of 'Said the Fly'

I loved this book — it's lyrical, languid, atmospheric, uniquely sensual.

Dusty-Anne Rhodes, author of 'Hard'

The Company of Men pulls us immediately into a world where the windows are too tall for anyone to escape from, the chair positioning too lonely, and where no one dances to the pianist's music. Infused with the languid, laid-back atmosphere of a time from not-so-long-ago, the story reminds one to reach for that glass of lemonade and go sit in the sun for a while.

Abha Iyengar, author of 'Flash Bites' and 'Shrayan'

The Company of Men

The Company of Men

of Men

a fictional memoir

Luisa Brenta

Pure
Slush

Find *Pure Slush* at http://pureslush.webs.com

All queries re *Pure Slush* can be made via email
to edpureslush@live.com.au

All *Pure Slush* books and eBooks can be bought
at http://pureslush.webs.com/store.htm

To my son

It's for him, that I first imagined
a naturally hospitable world.

The first problem for all of us,
men and women,
is not to learn, but to unlearn.

Gloria Steinem

Contents

Swallows 15

Company 17

Sinking pebbles 37

The linen room 54

Pearls 64

Late in the season 77

Renovations 87

Pendulum 98

Letters 105

Opening 113

Swallows

My Grandmother's world comes back to me in curiously still flashes, as if I had been taking pictures, long ago, and they had turned yellow and brown through the years. It's pictures of her face — as in one of those French lessons with her that had become compulsory when I turned ten. Grandmother would collect her mouth around a French Ü and look as if she was going to produce an egg from the wrong orifice.

I see an overexposed picture of those large windows opening high onto the two-story salon, framing the waves of swallows that still stormed the Milanese sky at the time, turning my boredom into a nameless longing for escape.

And I follow my ten-year-old mind as it wanders from the boring French dialogue that Grandmother wants me to memorize, into the large room that always seems so familiar and yet so puzzling. Why have they put the windows so high? You can't reach them. You can see the sky, and the swallows; nobody can open those windows to find out what they look out onto. Why did they think they needed tall windows in the first place, then?

("Repetez, Mademoiselle. Bonjour Monsieur. Nous avons retenu deux chambres ici à l'hôtel." ... Oh no, the dialogue at the hotel reception — again. This time we maintain that we had reserved two rooms, in the stupid hotel.)

There is a fireplace, under the large mirror. I have never seen a fire in it. There are two armchairs against the opposite wall. A mahogany, crystal-topped coffee table keeps them apart. Two people would feel lonely in those chairs. That's why Grandmother has those large formal parties, I guess — where the pianist faces yet another wall, alone, and nobody brings him a glass of something, and nobody would ever dream of dancing to his music.

(... "Oui, Monsieur, c'etait bien deux chambres contigues." – Seems that we wanted adjoining rooms.)

I wonder if the party guests actually notice the long slates of alternating black and white marble that draw you from the entrance into the salon, toward the terrace, and then stop and point up to the tall, tall windows. If the guests did notice, they would come up to the terrace and then turn around, and see the red granite stairs ready to fly them up past the piano landing and on to the second floor. Up there the tall windows would finally be on their same level; but still unreachable – as they would find out – across the chasm of the salon, on the opposite wall.

("Mais enfin, on avait bien écrit qu'on voulait deux chambres avec panorama!" ... And, we wanted a view! What are windows good for, if you can't look out onto something?)

Everything in Grandmother's salon points up to the tall windows – and then welcomes you back into somber security once you are aware the windows cannot be reached, unless you want to fly.

Or have to.

Company

Every second and fourth afternoon of the week, Grandmother "orders the car" so that Gigi, her driver, handyman and waiter, can drive her to her bridge afternoon. That is with lady friends whose lives are as purposefully useless as her own. She refers to them by their last names – as in "the Bertolotti," or "the Mazzanti."

She calls Gigi by his first name; and it is Gigi – not Jiji, à la Française – Djidji, à la Milanaise; short for Luigi. Grandmother has actually chosen that name for him; none of us knows what Gigi's real name is. I have asked him once, but the grown-ups were around and I was told to "leave the servants alone, let them do their work in peace."

Three times a year – before each of Grandmother's three yearly holidays, twice on the Riviera and once in the Alps – Gigi is told to put the car through a complete check-up. Gigi loves this job, you can tell, and we, the children, love to sneak off to the garage and watch Gigi coax the engine into furious sounds, with touches of his magic tools. Gigi smiles at my little brother and me; he explains what he is doing and gives us licorice. Also, he is always first to know when grown-ups are approaching; then he suddenly raises his voice and tells us to go back to our homework, let him get La Signora's car ready in time. But he winks at us as he says so.

At dinner, as Gigi waits at the table in a white jacket and white gloves, Grandmother asks about the car. "She runs like a deer and sounds like a violin," Gigi always answers. I wonder why he sticks to this phrase. It only gives Grandmother one extra source of wrath when the car eventually breaks down, yet again, on the way to Portofino.

In the summer of '63, I am stuck with the assignment of "keeping Grandmother company" on her way to the Riviera; my parents and younger brother will meet us there in three days. Our whole family is expected to visit Grandmother at least once on each of her three annual vacations; we the children find this a very unpleasant duty, given the number of rules and regulations that haunt the life of the young in all of Grandmother's homes.

As I look back at that trip, I see myself sitting beside Grandmother on the backseat of the Aurelia Gran Turismo. Grandmother is dozing off – still sitting somehow perfectly straight, hands weighed down in her lap by several cameo rings. She could be dead and set in marble – were it not for the heavy breaths from her half-open mouth – just short of snoring.

I'm bored. I can't talk to Gigi – Grandmother would wake up instantly and tell me not to distract the driver from his task. It's so hot in the car. The seats smell of leather and cigars. I count the buttons in the upholstery and lightly punch one after the other, half hoping for some kind of mechanical reaction — a secret passage that suddenly opens into the air, over the meadows that unfold beyond the closed car window.

We're now slowing down, for no apparent reason. We're still far from the coast. I pull myself up and kneel on the car seat ("Feet off the upholstery!") to look beyond Gigi's head at the road before us. I am actually hoping for a hold-up ... That would at least let me peep into people's cars, maybe pull faces at other children trapped behind other car windows ...

No traffic in sight. But our car coughs a couple of times — and then stops.

I look at Gigi's face in his rear mirror. He returns my look — head not moving, face blank. I go back to my proper sitting position — and freeze. We wait.

Grandmother jolts; she opens her eyes and looks left and right, and then left and right again and says, "What ... ? What ... ?" Then she opens her eyes some more.

"GIGI."

Gigi turns to face her pursed lips and raised eyebrow (only one eyebrow — how does Grandmother do that?). Gigi turns very slowly, and opens a wide smile over his incomplete collection of yellow teeth.

"Signora."

Grandmother's face is a perfectly still mask; her gaze is fixed on a distant point behind Gigi's face. She doesn't speak; she's waiting for guilty Gigi to utter his response one more time. Gigi lets her wait too, but not really too long, just a fraction of a minute longer than his position grants him. Guilty beyond any reasonable doubt.

"Ma'am?"

"Gigi, open my door." Gigi gets out of the car on one side and walks around it to the rear car-door on the other.

Grandmother gets out, turns her back on us and stands as if looking at the sea in the distance. Gigi stands to attention one step behind her, looking in her same direction. Until she turns and suddenly, irrevocably, loses her composure.

"Gigi Gigi Gigi!" She stamps her foot and throws her ringed hands in the air, raises her voice, goes red in the face, as she showers Gigi with a volley of shockingly "common" insults. Gigi keeps perfectly still, expressionless in the face of his Signora's unseemly explosion.

Then she catches herself. She stammers, looks left and right again, and finally makes for her usual strategic exit — she closes her eyes, tilts her head back and very slowly slumps along the closed car door.

Gigi steps forward just in time to catch her, then looks at me to indicate that I should now open the car door. He lies her down on the backseat of the car, with her shins in my lap. He hands me the folded map of Liguria with which I am now supposed to fan Grandmother, until she decides to open her eyes.

Not a word is spoken. I start fanning and Gigi walks to the front of the car, and opens the engine hood. Gigi works away at the engine. The engine mutters away, occasionally coughs; but it does not roar here as it did in the garage. Not any more
…

Grandmother and Grandpa Federico also have a villa in the mountains; another place which we have to visit once every summer – for the most boring days of the whole vacation.

At the end of the Fifties, Grandpa and Grandmother had established a summer residence in Grandpa's native village – a spot soon to become quite a chic vacation resort thanks to the numerous luxury homes that Grandpa himself would build for the newly rich of the prosperous Italian Sixties. However, rather than occupying one of the first recently built villas, they have bought an old and established one, on Via Garibaldi, only a few meters from the village square and the new 'Caffè Aperitivo'.

The villa looks like a pretty chalet and it is blessed with permanent chilly humidity, even when it isn't raining (and it usually rains here throughout August). The kitchen and the living room actually share the same mixture of household smells: dish wash, washing detergent and stale bread – in a blend with food from last night, burned wood from the fireplace and sometimes chocolate.

My great-grandmother, Bisnonna, always spends that vacation with us, in her room under the roof. This is where the servants lived – "before the war, when everything was different." Grandmother has put Bisnonna up there, no doubt, to ensure that it takes a lot of steps, and the sound of several squeaking stairs, before she can make it down to the main living room and embarrass the guests with that daily report on her bowel movements. Even I can see that Bisnonna makes these reports on purpose for some guests — a special edition with enriched details when the Bertolottis are here. She does not like the Bertolottis. "A well-assorted couple, though," she told me once, "she looks like a dressed-up prostitute, and he like a pimp. It all hangs together nicely, as it should."

At age seventy-four, Bisnonna has long been a widow; Great-grandpa famously left her without a penny, when he died of a stroke in somebody else's bed, decades ago. Bisnonna has been taken into her daughter's home "out of charity and filial duty," as Grandmother never tires of explaining.

I can still see myself climbing the stairs to Bisnonna's room on the Day of the Storm — but well before the Storm actually happens. Halfway up I already know she is awake — from the squeak of the wooden floor under her rocking chair.

I knock and go in. She is crocheting — she always is, when not busy embarrassing the guests. Today, she is making yet another white tablemat. These white tablemats and several smaller coasters are all over her room, every one of them placed neatly under something that sits on ugly furniture.

"Come in, Young One. I must tell you something, and it is urgent." She doesn't stop crocheting, nor looks up at me. I sit on the floor — in Bisnonna's room this is allowed.

"Mark my words, Young One. Never ever throw yourself away. Never give up on that one. No matter what."

"Throw myself away?" I'm used to Bisnonna's sudden edicts, and I have long since learned to wait for more.

"Someday, they will try to marry you off to some fat bag-of-money who looks like Bertolotti. Only fatter, mark my words." She looks up from the crochet and raises her eyebrows (both of them) at me. "Don't you go throwing yourself away. Don't let them talk you into it."

"Bisnonna, they don't marry people off anymore. Only in the movies."

"That's what you think. I was married off to Costante, God rest his sinner's soul, when I was sixteen."

"I'm not sixteen, Bisnonna."

"Better start worrying about it right away. Better beware." She raises her eyebrows at me again.

"I'll marry whoever I want to marry."

"That's what you think now. That's what you will think then − they'll make you believe it all right. Then you will be married. Then pregnant. Then Fat-Bag-of-Money takes another woman. He knows you will stay with the children. He knows you will bring them up, even if he's busy elsewhere, because he knows you're smart. He doesn't want one who is smarter than him, though, unless it doesn't show, that's why he has married you before you go to college or something. But instead, you must go to college or something, d'you hear me, you do not throw yourself away."

"Lotti!" from downstairs. "Lotti, where are you? We are off to La Colombella, we are late already!"

"Coming!"

La Colombella is the local "Country Club." They call it a Country Club, although it's in the mountains. It's a place where the men play bocce and drink; the women play bridge. They also have parties there – with the Blue Dove Swing Band, a name like in American movies – but only grown-ups can go.

Except today – today is Family Day at La Colombella, which means the men will play bocce and drink, the women will be playing bridge, and the children will take care of themselves and come up with something to do that will not be noisy.

Bisnonna looks up from her crochet once more and says, "You'd better take an umbrella, Young One." Then, unexpectedly, she smiles. Her eyes go back to her work. As I leave her room I hear her rocking chair creaking on the floorboards again.

Here we are at La Colombella. I am bored stiff, sitting in an armchair in the Card Players' Salon. No other children around – not yet, at least. Grandpa says they were scared back into their living rooms by the grey clouds out to the East, over Mount Baldo. I look out of the tall window toward Mount Baldo and I do see the clouds – not grey though: dark green.

Anyway, I sit in this armchair in the Card Players' Salon, where Grandmother and her lady friends are playing Canasta. "Sit there like a good girl and wait for your friends," she has said. I try. I practice tapping 'Frère Jacques' with my left-hand on the armrest – I can usually do it with my right-hand only; then I try it with my left foot. I slouch slowly but surely into a pool of apathy – until Grandmother sees me from the card table and tells me to sit up straight and be a lady.

The afternoon light dims slowly and I'm almost ready to die by holding my breath while I count to two hundred. At last, I hear something, from the conversation at the card table that sounds interesting. It usually is, when it's the Bertolotti who is speaking (yes, that Bertolotti), as she tends to forget "there are children in the room" and says things that make the other women giggle and blush. Today it's about Maria Poletti — I remember her; I went to her wedding three years ago and wore a pink dress with a crown of little flowers on my head.

"Of course she shows it off when she gets the chance — at tennis matches included, how's that for bad taste? It's all she has left. And she didn't even get it from him — not really. It's her engagement ring, comes from his family. Married three years to that kind of money and not even the villa in Santa Margherita to her name. You wouldn't believe it, she actually has nothing but her monthly allowance. She's had to sell the Alfa Romeo — a wedding present, you know, he hadn't been able to get out of that. Now, what was on the woman's mind through her wedded years, I cannot imagine."

"It's not entirely her fault, come on. She was so young. She had no idea what was going on — his having had that lover forever, and no intention of letting go of her, either. Everybody knew but the bride-to-be, remember? She was young. Romantic. And she was never in a position to get anything out of him, not even at the start. He couldn't have cared less, poor girl. And she never got pregnant, you know, that just has to mean something. So it was not entirely her fault. And it's not as if she didn't know on which side her bread was buttered. It's not as if she didn't know how to provide for her future. She was just never really in a position to do anything."

"Well, be that as it may, she never reacted, never fought back. Never even tried, to get rid of the other woman. She spent her first year of marriage like a recluse – and whenever she did show up at anything, she sported blue circles under red eyes – how could anyone find that attractive? She let herself go, she gave up. What if we all gave up when they start spending the night out? And I don't mean in one of those houses; I mean when they start to spend nights in the same house. Not at a Madam's, like all of their friends. You know. That would be the time to worry, right? But by then, if we've played our cards well, we are at least financially safe – not reduced to begging from our fathers, like Donata's daughter."

"Yes," says Grandmother, with a faint smile. "By our third anniversary I already had our first villa to my name. And a couple of interesting rings. Yes." She hasn't raised her eyes from the cards, but her demure smile is still there.

The others exchange quick looks. Then they sigh. "Well. Poor girl."

"Yes. Poor girl."

It's really dark in the cards room now; too dark, really, for three o'clock. And the sky through the tall window is really green, dark green, and even yellow here and there. Grandmother is ringing the little silver bell that always sits on the table, to call in the waiter from the bar and have him turn on the light. The switch is right by the door. I jump from my

26

chair to turn on the light myself — grateful to have something to do for thirty seconds — but Grandmother tells me to get back to my chair. It is not for me to turn on the lights at La Colombella. So I turn off the lights that I had already turned on and I'm back in my chair, while Grandmother is growing impatient because the bartender hasn't come in from the next room and she has had to ring twice already.

Suddenly we hear the French windows in the next room slamming open, and the sound of broken glass. Then a bang, and more noise from outside. It's getting cold — the wind is blowing in from the next room. The women at Grandma's table do not get up to see what's happened, so I also sit. They look at each other tentatively and then surreptitiously at Grandmother. She seems not to have noticed and is making a big show of her impatience at the absent bartender — sighing, and rolling her eyes, and ringing the silver bell again and again. We hear another window bang and more glass crashing and the ladies all stand up now — even Grandmother. They exchange looks but no one moves until the men come rushing into the room. They have left the bocce court in a hurry and they have run into the basement where they expected to find the ladies. They have seen that four of them are missing, and Grandmother's granddaughter with them. Now they voice their relief as they find them in the Card Players' Salon; they yell at us, they grab everybody by the arms and practically shove us, and the ladies' little shrill cries, down the hall and into the basement. Grandmother puts up mild resistance in an attempt to go back and grab the silver bell — as a matter of principle, I guess — but Grandpa grabs her again and drags her out the room. She does say, "Federico, you forget your manners. What are you doing? What is this?" but gets no answer and ends up squeezed into the basement with everybody else, just before the men close the door and bolt it by shoving past her and her offended expression.

The noise outside is terrifying now. I'm afraid of storms, especially when the thunderbolts explode in your ears and you don't even have that half a second of suspense between brightness and cracking – you don't see the lightning from the basement and you can't put your hands over your ears in time. I crunch in a corner with my arms around my head and wait for it to stop but it doesn't, it's furious. It keeps making loud, horrible noises and you can hear but not see. Nobody says a word here, not even Grandmother.

A very long half hour has passed by the time the Men unbolt the door and we all emerge.

Everything outside is perfectly still now, as if it had been still for decades. The hall is incredibly bright and cold, and almost empty of furniture; the tornado has blown off the roof and even snatched the Louis XIV chairs that were lining the walls. Broken glass everywhere, the smell of Pernod from yellow rivulets on the ground.

Later, we are driving home in the Gran Turismo – fast, as we are thinking of Bisnonna who's been home alone through the whole storm. We're all silent until Grandpa says, "I do hope that your mother is safe," to Grandmother.

"If she has had the good sense to go downstairs rather than sit right under the roof doing her silly crocheting," she answers, keeping her eyes on the road ahead.

Everybody is silent again; Grandmother's shoulders are especially silent, and I can sense her pursed lips even if I can't see them from the back seat.

But then she speaks again. "You sure took your sweet time coming to our rescue at the club."

Grandpa waits a little too long to answer, then says, "What were you ladies doing in the Card Players' room anyway? We expected to find you in the basement with everybody else – we had to look for you when we saw that you were missing!"

Another few long seconds of silence.

"You would have known where we were, had you been inside like anybody with any sense, with a storm approaching," Grandmother says. "But, of course, a game of cards with the ladies can never be as much fun for you as a silly game of whatever it was with anybody else. Of course. Anybody else but your own wife."

Grandpa keeps quiet this time.

"Do you think that people don't notice? You are never in the same room with me. Not even in public. People talk."

Grandpa still keeps silent. Grandmother doesn't give up: "People talk as they did last summer when Maria Bertolotti's chambermaid showed up in church with a coral bracelet, of all things, and everybody knows that Bertolotti himself has no use for anything young and pretty since after the operation, and guess who only has to go through the garden hedge to reach the servants' sheds in the Bertolottis' garden, and ..."

"E-NOUGH!" Grandpa slams his hands on the wheel and really raises his voice now. "That stupid story again! You are obsessed, that's what you are. We are driving home to your mother after what's been happening, and you can't think of anything better than bringing up that stupid story!" He slams his hands on the wheel again. "That stupid story again."

Another silence sets in. I keep as still as I can, alone on the back seat.

As we come to the gate of the villa and Gigi rushes out of the garage to let us in, Grandmother says something under her breath and Grandpa slams on the wheel for the third time. Then turns and looks at her with his whole head and his whole body and I think he's going to hit her, but he doesn't. We get out of the car and I don't know what Grandmother has said to Grandpa.

When we get inside I run upstairs, of course – more afraid as I pass yet another broken window on the second landing. Somebody yells "careful of the broken glass" from downstairs – but I have to dash upstairs and bang the door open.

And there she is, Bisnonna, "sitting right under the roof" – or what is left of it. Perfectly straight in her rocking chair, eyes closed, wet locks hanging from the pins in her chignon. A newly-blue sky pours its light into her room. The mountain sun is there again – to dry her hair. Her kentia is on the floor; pot shattered and wet soil around it. White crochet coasters are scattered all over the place – they must have been flying in the storm like mountain gulls.

But everything is settled now, and still. I too, freeze at the door.

This is when Bisnonna opens her eyes and — without turning her head — looks around. Her eyes reach my face and rest on me as if they needed some time to come back and recognize me. They are focusing very, very slowly. Then she smiles, for the second time that same day.

Later, as I'm leaving her room, she stops me at the door: "Young One."

"Yes, Bisnonna."

"You are still not allowed to throw yourself away in the future. Have I made myself clear, Young One?"

Back in Milan, and throughout the year, Sunday Luncheon at Grandmother's is, of course, compulsory. There are times when my brother and I — and the Parents, I suspect — would want to go on a Sunday trip — to see families who are spending the weekend at their country homes, who have children we could play with — but we can't, as we have to show up at Grandmother's at 12.00 sharp, dressed in what she still calls "Church attire", because we are supposed to have been in Church before we come for lunch.

Gigi opens the door; he always greets my father with a large smile, then goes back to the kitchen where he is busy fitting the Sunday chicken and potatoes onto a plate that is much too small for the meal, but is solid silver and therefore must be used on Sundays.

We always find Grandmother in the two-story salon, sitting in the armchair where she "receives". She does not get up, but protrudes her head slightly to offer her forehead to my father's kiss; then she turns her cheek, for Mother and each of us children. We the children know that we will sit there, listening to adult conversation, until Gigi appears in a white jacket and white gloves to say, "Lunch is served, Ma'am."

This is the only occasion when children are allowed into the dining-room — which is a pity, because it's the brightest room in the home. The floor is shiny parquet and the three large windows are level with you — even level with my ten-year-old head. You can look outside and see a lot of what is there — the flowers on the terrace, mainly snapdragons — with a friendly look and a scary name; but also dahlias. The light suddenly floods your face when you come in from the dark salon; it always seems to me that it laughs happily at catching you unprepared.

Against the wall on your right there is that long piece of furniture that Grandmother calls "the console" — famous within the family for harboring "chocolates that are meant for guests." Grandmother is always afraid that someone will steal the chocolates; that's why she locks them up in the console and leaves them there to wait for the rightful consumers. As she does not see fit to bring them out during one of her formal parties ("Chocolate is way too expensive to give it away to just anybody — and then, fruit jellies and pastry mignon are what everybody would rather have, aren't they?"), the chocolates sit in their hideaway for months. When they finally reappear, they are covered with a whitish coat that betrays their age.

My brother Alberto and I are young enough to want any chocolate, and sometimes we are promised one praline for the end of the meal, if we behave through it. But we never make it through ...

... "Stop swinging your legs under the table, Carlotta. Do sit properly. Sit up, I said. And show your wrists. That's right. You don't want anybody to think that you are hiding your hands because you didn't wash them properly for lunch, do you?" That is my mother, whispering; but not in an unfriendly way.

"And you don't want anybody to think that you are scratching your tummy under the table, do you?"— My father this time, aloud, with a wink.

"Aldo, please!"— Grandmother.

I am by now so sure the scene will be repeated every Sunday, with little or no variation, that I make a point of starting to swing my legs and leaving my hands in my lap as soon as I am seated at the table. I find it so reassuring, this repetition. And it gives me such a feeling of power, being able to produce the expected reaction, with the expected words, and from a number of adults in rapid succession.

However, today my brother Alberto is about to perform his famous Curtain Routine in Grandmother's dining room, thereby making a permanent mark in family folklore.

"May I get up? I need to blow my nose," Alberto says.

"You do not mention blowing your nose at the lunch table."

"May I get up?"

"You may."

"I forgot my handkerchief."

"Typical," Grandmother says. "Aldo, I told you before, that it's time for Alberto to be required to wear a coat to Sunday Lunch. Now, that would also provide him with a breast pocket in which to carry a handkerchief. And he would be able to use it more discreetly. Possibly once before lunch, as a precaution to avoid having to leave the table in the middle of a meal."

"I don't have a handkerchief," says Alberto.

"For Heaven's sake, get up and solve the problem!" Grandmother is exasperated; not yet indignant, as she doesn't know what's coming.

Alberto looks around the table with that lovely smile of his — a smile that hides a rascal's soul behind an angel's face, at six. He lays the linen napkin neatly by his dish, slides off his chair, goes to the window that opens unto the terrace, and fakes blowing his nose in the silk curtains.

The sound is loud and quite realistic. Mother, Father and I are already familiar with the performance: Alberto has been practicing at home; he faked it in Nanny's apron once. Nanny started screaming and jumping around and that's how Alberto and I were sure it worked. Also, he and I were both punished for that — he for doing it and I for laughing.

But I guess this time Father is the one who will go without his Sunday ice-cream: after ten seconds during which his face has turned purple, he has finally looked up at Grandmother's face and burst out laughing. He can't stop; it looks as though he's going to fall off his chair. Guess that gives me the right to laugh, too? Mother keeps a straight face a little longer, then puts the napkin in front of her face, but you can hear the muffled sound and see her shoulders shaking until she finally gives up too and laughs and laughs. Grandpa looks around the table, speechless, until he suddenly seems to get it, and not only starts to laugh but also to slap Grandmother's back and his own thigh, alternately. The whole table is roaring, except for Grandmother. Gigi has come in, carrying the cheese plate, just in time to witness the scene. He takes everything in at a glance and dashes out immediately – but we hear the sound of laughter from the kitchen, and other sounds too, he must have dropped something as he was doubling over.

Grandmother is sitting tight in her salt-statue stance as she beholds Sodom and Gomorrah. When general laughter subsides, she says, "Now, this is definitely unacceptable." Grandpa roars again. Alberto opens his eyes wide and says, "Oh I'm sorry, does this mean Gigi will need to wash the curtains right away?"

Grandmother stands up and overturns her chair as she leaves the room.

Nobody is laughing any more, with the exception of Father, whose eyes are carefully turned down, away from us. I know we all are in trouble; last time Grandmother left the Sunday table she stayed in her room for three days. She "refused food and drink," as the maid was instructed to tell my father when he called and was not granted access to the lady of the house. I was not as worried as the Parents seemed to be then. It was obvious to me Grandma was drinking as much as she wanted from the faucet in her private bathroom and, as for food, when she had opened her toilette's main drawer with me in the room I had seen the boxes of "fine chocolates" she kept in there. There were three boxes at least — she thought I couldn't see them, as she was careful to sit at the toilette right in the way of my gaze.

But this time there is actually good reason to worry; after twenty-four hours Grandmother has stopped answering the maid from behind the closed door. After two days Father is called in to shoulder the door open. Grandmother is not there. Only a pink envelope is found; it smells of cologne and is addressed to Grandpa.

Sinking pebbles

I have long since learned to stay out of the way when adults raise their voices, pace the marble hall or wave off Gigi summoning them to dinner. I disappear in one of the lonely chairs opposite the unlit fireplace in the salon. Grandpa is in the parlor with Father and Mother, and he is actually yelling.

"How could she do this to me, what the hell do I tell people when they ask? How could she jeopardize everything – our social position, even the bloody business, everything I've been working for, all these years? Who does she think she is?"

"Grandfather, please, the children can hear ..." – my mother.

"Who in bloody hell DOES she think she is!" – even louder – "And I don't care WHO hears, and don't you dare shush me! Who the hell does she think she is, after I practically married her out of the gutter, where she was soon to be if she hadn't found an idiot like me to put up with her bloody lady's airs all these years, and her pretenses. And her jealousy. On top of everything else!"

Mother and Father are whispering something to him, but I can't hear what. I'm not really paying attention anymore. I'm not even as scared as I usually am when Grandpa stops smiling and suddenly looks so mean and red in the face. I can hear that he's being mean and red in the other room, but I've sunk into my own thoughts. It's clear by now Grandmother has not been taken by someone for ransom, like that movie on TV. And those men our parents told us to watch out for, the ones who want to give you candy, they steal children only. And she isn't dead, I think. So, what happened?

Mother comes out of the parlor, and startles when she sees me.

"Lotti! What are you doing here?"

"Waiting. You told me to wait. That we couldn't go home just now, but soon."

"Go ... please go help Gigi and Agata in the kitchen while you wait."

Go help Gigi? Now, this is a first. Does she mean that I actually have permission to go distract the servants from their work?

I get up from the armchair and dash, before she changes her mind.

Today the kitchen is going to be particularly interesting, because Agata is there. Agata is Gigi's wife. She comes over as extra help twice a week, but we don't get to see much of her as she usually stays in the linen room, next to the pantry. She irons or sews and she smiles whenever one of us children manages to sneak in in spite of the usual instruction to "leave the servants alone." She smiles today also, but looks surprised to see me.

"Well, look who's here! Where have you been all afternoon?" she says, "You've been as quiet as a mouse, I didn't even know that you were still visiting your grandparents!" Gigi appears at the door of the linen room.

She looks at her husband, eyes open larger than usual in a worried question mark.

I say, "Visiting Grandpa, you mean."

Agata does not reply. She considers the expression on my face, looks into my eyes, which I try to keep as blank as I can. Then she gives Gigi another meaningful look and turns her face away from me, as if wanting to think again before she speaks. She turns to me again, "Are you worrying over your grandmother?"

"No."

"No?"

"I've seen the letter."

"You have seen the letter!"

"Not read the letter. I mean I've seen that it was there, that's how I know that Grandmother hasn't been kidnapped and that she hasn't died like old Mrs. Lanti from next door, and that she's only gone somewhere. And I'm not worried that she'll get hungry without dinner because I know that she has chocolate to eat if she gets hungry — I know she always has chocolate in her room that she thinks I don't know about, so I'm sure she took the chocolate with her and she's not hungry."

"I see."

"Grandpa has been yelling."

Gigi cuts in. "I'll have to fix that car, you know, Agata," he speaks louder than usual, "before it gets too late in the day. I've had problems with the carburetor again." Turns to me: "Would you like to come to the garage? Maybe you can hold the torch for me."

I gladly follow Gigi to the garage. In the garage I don't hold the torch but sit on the wooden table and swing my legs. Gigi works and keeps silent.

I have a sudden idea. I guess it's from looking at Gigi working at the engine. "I know where I would go if I were Grandmother. I mean, if I didn't know where to go. If I didn't have anything urgent to do. I would go straight to Portofino and stay at the Hotel, and get up early in the morning so that I could get the peach crostata for breakfast before the tall man gets up and eats most of it."

Gigi stops working and turns to look at me a little too fast – he bangs his head against the hood. He doesn't even swear under his breath, as I have heard him do sometimes before. He is studying my face. I must have said something interesting. So I keep going:

"And I would stay at the hotel, it's so much better than the villa. I wouldn't stay at the villa in Santa Margherita, if I were Grandmother, because there's no one there and I would feel lonely. I would stay at the hotel and say 'Yes' when other guests say, 'Would you join me for a walk to the reef in the afternoon?' That's what I would do, if I were Grandmother."

Seeing Gigi work at the engine of the car must have made me think of this. I remember one morning at the Portofino hotel, the morning after the car stopped on the way to the coast and Grandmother was so upset.

The sun had been so warm that morning in Portofino, so delicate – it touched you as if it was just passing by. Nothing like the sunshine in Milan, that was not there most of the year and then burst out of the grey clouds to steam your head in the sudden July heat. The sunshine caressing your face was the only good thing about having to accompany Grandmother to Portofino alone.

No, not the only good thing, actually. The hotel in Portofino was much better than the villa in Santa Margherita. That year, Grandmother had had tenants for the winter, and they had asked to stay an extra month. She still had to take her regular vacation at her regular time of the year. Portofino, and its luxurious hotel, had been chosen as a substitute. I loved this hotel; there was much more going on than at the villa: people coming and going and sitting out on the long, long terrace overlooking the garden and the sea, and having strange conversations, making pleasant, reassuring murmurs, along the terrace, which were carried away by the passing sunlight.

The restaurant was more interesting still. For one thing, some of the dishes that people chose to eat I had never seen before, and went by such exotic names as "carottes Julienne"– which meant that you wanted your carrots grated in sort of tiny slices, instead of the usual way. Grandmother was particularly fond of carottes Julienne; she always insisted that they should be "Julienne", and she always sent the dish back when she got what she called "... common grated carrots, and I said Julienne – Julienne, understand? And now you will have to carry this back to the kitchen, as I specifically asked for carottes Julienne and I am not having grated carrots instead just to please you." The waiter did not seem particularly displeased, nor did he seem to have a problem taking the "common carrots" back to the kitchen; it wasn't his restaurant, after all.

Grandmother would not make much conversation at the table; rather, she would be looking around in that funny way of hers, moving her eyes all over the place without moving her head. You wouldn't have been able to say that she was looking at the other tables, had you not been right in front of her, where I was sitting. I always wondered how she did that and tried it myself a couple of times, but I guess I ended up being more obvious than she was. She caught me and said, "Now Carlotta what are you doing, pulling faces at the dinner table, you don't want the other guests to think that you were born cross-eyed, do you? Nor to infer that you don't know how a young lady should behave."

Best of all was when a meal was served outside, on the terrace.

The morning after the car incident, I had expected Grandmother to stay in her room, and I had hurried to the terrace as soon as I knew that breakfast service would start; I had been looking forward to choosing a table and sitting there alone ("Sit up straight, Carlotta") and being called Signorina and talked of in the third person, as in "What can I bring the Signorina this morning?" I knew that Royalty was spoken of in the third person — at least in that TV show, An Evening at Family Theatre, that the Parents let me watch on Saturday nights and which had given me this fantasy about really being a princess even though my family was hiding this fact from me "to avoid the child growing up to be conceited." Probably Grandmother had forgotten to warn the waiters in the hotel about this. Plus, if I really was a princess, that would explain that grown-up obsession about my sitting up straight — I mean, I had to be trained to balance a crown on my head with no apparent effort. I was even ready to try and sit up straight, in view of my future duties.

On this particular morning, when I came out onto the terrace I was surprised to see Grandmother already there. She hadn't stayed in her room and she didn't look like she had "one of my migraines." She was looking at the garden and when she turned to hear me say, "Good morning Grandmother," she had ... a smile on her face. That was the first time that I had ever seen Grandmother smile in the morning. I was so surprised that I probably paused too long before the next expected sentence, which was of course, "Did you have a good night, Grandmother?" She noticed, and let the smile go before she answered, "Yes, thank you Carlotta, and I hope the same is true of you."

Guests were arriving to sit at other tables, most of them couples; none of them with children, unluckily. Only a few were alone, but still looked like they were waiting to be joined by someone from their room upstairs. But the tall man two tables away did not look like he was waiting for someone; he had the morning paper with him, and was trying to attract the waiter's attention. You could tell that he was tall even though he was sitting down. He looked old, to me, older than Father, almost as old as Grandmother; and I was positive by now he had no grandchildren with him. I lost interest until I noticed the waiter was taking him a plate with two whole slices of that peach crostata I planned to order for myself, and started worrying that other hotel guests could also be served before me and finish the crostata. Grandmother had turned again towards the garden and seemed to have forgotten all about nodding to the next waiter.

"Grandmother," I dared to whisper at one point "... Grandmother?"

She turned her head toward me slowly; and she was smiling again, of all things! But she caught herself much sooner this time.

"Grandmother, should we order?"

She paused for a moment and rather than rebuking me and giving the usual lecture on the value of patience, just said, "Yes, Carlotta, I suppose we could."

She nodded to the waiter and ordered her customary morning yoghurt, and a cappuccino; but to my great surprise she also said, "... and please bring a double serving of crostata for the Signorina. Two slices on a large plate."

I was speechless. Grandmother was definitely not angry any more; the car incident seemed to have been forgotten in a much shorter time than Grandmother usually took to forget. She looked unexpectedly ... well, her lips were not so thin any more. She looked a little like Agata when she had finished the ironing, with all the ironing things put away, and was sitting in the linen room, hands in her lap, a faint smile as she looked out of the window and waited for Gigi to finish cleaning the kitchen and take her home during his lunch break.

My slices of crostata were served, and eaten as fast as my Signorina status allowed; Grandmother ate very slowly and still seemed occupied with whatever fantasy the view of the garden had to offer her this morning. I had been swinging my legs for a while now, to no avail; I finally asked to be excused.

Grandmother turned once more towards me; she looked at me as if from afar; then looked at the unfinished breakfast on her plate. I knew what that was bound to mean, "You should know better than asking to be excused when I am still eating and you shouldn't eat so fast it's not good for you and it's not ladylike." But the sentence never came. Grandmother nodded her permission and I even got away with jumping from the table. I was off into the garden and hopping down the alley towards the belvedere.

The belvedere was another one of my favorite spots at the hotel; as its name announced – belvedere, "beautiful seeing" – you could sit there and watch the boats at sea – a few fishing boats, many more yachts, at that time of the year. Or you could imagine my friend the Blue Princess walking up the alley with her fiancé the Prince, dragons and mean stepmothers years behind them in the lazy, bright morning of their happily ever after.

Or you could even look back at the terrace where the grownups were taking a whole hour for breakfast. And there was Grandmother, in her white summer dress. She was still sitting at her table, a hand raised to shade her eyes from the sun; she was looking up at another guest – the tall man who had started on the crostata before me. He was now standing by her chair, Panama hat in hand, talking to her.

She was laughing.

"What is this about Portofino, now?" says Gigi, immediately turning back to the car's engine, as if my answer couldn't really interest him more than so much.

Ok, I don't answer; instead I jump off the bench and look into the engine too. Gigi works on the car engine for a while and then turns his head from under the car's bonnet – just his head, to look at me straight in the face. "Do not, do you hear me, do NOT go bothering your parents, or Grandpa, with these stories of yours, Miss Lotti." And then, softer, suddenly softer, "They are in pain, Miss Lotti. You don't want to attract attention, waste their time, and make it worse, with these stories of yours." He looks down at the engine as if about to go back to it, but instead he turns and gazes once more. "Are we agreed, Miss Lotti?"

I look at his serious face and nod. I promise. It is obvious that Gigi knows what has become of Grandmother; and that no one else does.

Bisnonna has stayed in her room throughout the commotion that has followed the discovery of Grandmother's absence and of the letter she has left. Here in Milan, Bisnonna lives in a room that opens onto the balcony overlooking the salon.

Grandpa isn't yelling anymore, but the grownups are still shut up in the study. Bisnonna emerges from her room and walks up and down the balcony – slowly back and slowly forth;

three beats to every step, chick-chick-thump, because she walks with a stick. I look up at her; she knows I'm there, of course — she usually does, unlike most grownups; she reminds me of Gigi, sometimes. She stops for a moment, looks down at me from above; then continues walking, chick-chick-thump.

The door of the study opens and out step Grandfather, Mother and Father. Mother sees me and says, "Lotti-what-are-you-doing-here?" for the second time in the last hour.

"You said I should wait and be quiet and that we would be going home a little later and that I should go help Gigi and Agata, so I did and then I came back here."

"Right," says Mother looking somewhere else, I don't know where, "Right, yes, we will do that now very soon. Right."

"Federico." Bisnonna from the balcony. "Federico." A pause. "Out of the gutter, my ass." (Oh my. She has actually said 'ass'.) She has Grandpa's attention, now.

"What?" Grandpa barks back. "What? WHAT?"

"Out of the gutter my ass. (Again.) I heard you. By the way, we all did." She glances at the chair where I am sitting, in the salon below. Grandpa looks at me as from another world, then drops his shoulders and looks confused for a few seconds, or embarrassed or something; but he flushes again as he looks up at Bisnonna — purple. "Do YOU have something to say? YOU?"

"I certainly do and I certainly expect you in my room right away. I know better than making a scene right here, like some people." She turns and walks back to her room, just a hint more slowly than she normally would.

Grandpa is dumbfounded. Then he burns very red in the face again, he looks around as if he is groping for air and finally bursts. "And since when do YOU have a say in this house? Since when do you earn your own bread, around here? Since when do you get away with these new airs and pretenses?"

"Since you started behaving like an asshole." A short pause. "Be a man and come to my room."

Grandpa takes a second before he realizes his mouth is hanging open. Then turns an indignant look on Mother and Father, who are just standing there, perfectly still; he looks up at the balcony again, pulls down his jacket and starts on his rigid way up the stairs.

One month later, Grandmother has not yet reappeared. But the world seems to be settling down without her; none of the grownups has made much of a fuss over the changes taking place in the home she has suddenly left behind – or put aside. Nobody mentions the possibility of Grandmother's return because nobody is mentioning Grandmother.

The house rules and regulations are disrupted, as is the traditional menu for family meals. After years of a carefully planned two-week schedule ("the only way to make sure that you do not happen to serve the same thing twice in the same fortnight"), the menu is left to Gigi's initiative; Gigi likes fish, so Grandfather, Bisnonna and their guests – luckily limited to family members, given the present circumstances

— are now at risk of feeling sick should they only go near the sea again.

But it is impossible to go on this way, for several good reasons. A regular social life has to be resumed as soon as possible — to stifle gossip, which has quickly started to spread. Mother is now the official hostess; it will fall upon her to steer the Tuesday-evening regular guests' conversation away from the one juicy piece of news that will otherwise inspire it: "You know, they say she is on vacation, but who is going to believe that? The season has not even started on the coast. And a health resort is also out of the question in March. March is when you still want to be in town, of all places — unless you 'must' be away ... Or worse, 'want' to ..." Knowing grins.

The need for a housekeeper is agreed upon — just for this period of time, of course; Grandmother will naturally want to resume her full duties as Lady of the House as soon as she comes back from her health vacation — totally recovered, we dare to hope. The choice falls upon Agata, Gigi's wife, who is untrained in this higher responsibility but is well-known to the family and can be trusted. Mother will train her in the basics of the household — in full respect of Grandmother's habits and preferences, of course, so that nothing will look altered in any way when Grandmother comes back from her vacation.

Three months later anybody who has seen this household before Grandmother's "vacation" would notice nothing particularly unusual. Silence closes up over Grandmother's absence like water over a sinking pebble. The two-week schedule for the menu is retrieved and its commandments restored. Grandmother's room and private bathroom have been locked up to ensure that "everything is in perfect order when Grandmother returns from her vacation." Her place at the dinner table, to the right of Grandpa, has not been taken by any other member of the family; instead the plates and silver have gradually spread out to cover up the gap Grandmother has left between the head of the family and the next family guest. Mother still sits on the other side of the table when we have dinner with Grandpa; and that happens more often now, as "we don't want him to feel too lonely during Grandmother's vacation."

One day I see Mother sit down beside him in the study: he has been reading with the door open. He has laid the paper in his lap and is looking at the opposite wall as if he could actually see something there. Mother sits there a while, very straight, before he notices. "Yes?"

He looks mildly surprised — not as he comes out of his daydream; rather, because Mother and he seldom speak directly to each other; even less, on Mother's initiative. She blushes.

"Just wondering how you are, Papa."

"Why?"

"Well, you know, wondering if you miss ... you know ... husbands do rely on their wives for a lot of things... you know, they are sort of used to having them around ... I was wondering if you miss Grandmother and wish she was back from her vacation already." Pause. "Which could be making you sad, of course."

He looks at her. She has definitely captured his attention, but his look is inquisitive, rather than warm. Then he smiles at the corners of his lips. He picks up his paper and it is to the paper that his answer is spoken. "No need to worry. I am quite satisfied with the way you manage the household in her absence, if that is what you are asking about."

Mother waits for more; but it doesn't come. "Thank you," she says. "I am glad that you are satisfied. Actually, though, I was not thinking of the household only. I was afraid you would feel a little lonely, you know ... miss the spouse, actually."

He turns towards her now, takes off his reading glasses. "You couldn't possibly be asking about ... my manly necessities, could you, young woman?"

"Oh no, Papa, oh no, no, I was not thinking of that, oh no, I wouldn't!" A pause; she blushes and shakes her head, "I wouldn't. I was thinking that maybe you missed the person, you know. The companion."

"Companion."

"Yes, that's what I meant when I said 'spouse'."

He keeps his eyes on her face for another moment. Then he smiles, and returns to his paper. "You are very young. Indeed."

Mother sits there, silent. His eyes are on the paper, the conversation over for good. Until he says, "Should you not be checking on Gigi in the kitchen? Dinner should have been served five minutes ago."

Mother stands up and walks to the kitchen.

Something has happened to Grandpa, though. He is not as witty as I have always known him to be, in his coarse way, nor laughing much. He laughed often, when Grandmother was around; mostly at her. Maybe now nothing amuses him, or not so often.

He had laughed at Grandmother's incredible Sunday hats, when he was ready for church and waiting for her in the salon. She would descend the stairs balancing one of those strange concoctions of ribbons and fruit — and one time a stuffed bird — on her head; he would be as obvious as possible about his efforts to stay serious, rolling his eyes at us; then, he would burst into loud laughter. She would stop halfway down the stairs, freezing her smile, clenching the rail with her left hand.

Or they would have arguments at dinner while we were all seated around the table, about the appearance of the vegetable gratin that had just been served, or something; she would look down at her plate not answering Grandpa's disparaging remarks on how the "kitchen staff" were being supervised; then she would lose her temper completely and actually yell, "You don't like anything I am or do!" He would then put on his famous 'very scared' look — gaping mouth, head sunk into his shoulders — push back his chair to 'run and hide', and disappear behind the dining-room door, from where he would soon show one arm waving a white handkerchief in mock surrender.

We all would laugh. Only Grandmother wouldn't; and I remember not understanding why, at the time.

But I miss Grandmother. While she was around, I never asked myself whether I had any real affection for her. Grandmother was there to be obeyed — that was clear — and not only by us children. I had not been really sure whether Grandpa had to obey her, or not: he didn't seem to give that many orders himself; but when he did, they were usually for her. Grandmother was also there to intrigue you — at least intrigue me. She was committed to a mysterious set of guidelines that needed not be mentioned directly but could not be overridden.

Most of all, I'm thinking more and more of that last vacation before Grandmother disappeared — the spring when I accompanied her to Portofino and I saw her laugh. I find my grandmother more interesting now than I ever have before. Her disappearance has cheated me of some unexpected insight — some fascinating revelation that her laughter in the Portofino morning air implied.

The linen room

Most of what I later learn about Grandmother never comes directly from her. My opportunity lies in the sudden visit of her sister Ada, and Ada's husband Rico. No one has told them what is going on. No one expected to ever see them again, as they have lived in America since way before the war; in the Sixties that still equals having moved to the moon for good.

Their stay is preceded by a phone call; but the phone call is made from their hotel in Milan, where they have spent their first night on Italian soil after so many years — and where they have no intention of spending another, of course, since they have relatives in the city and are surprising them at last with a long-overdue visit. It would be unforgiveable not to offer hospitality, no matter how inconvenient; it is also a matter of course to accept it. Aunt Ada and Uncle Rico therefore appear at the door one Wednesday morning, and shock Gigi who is answering the doorbell, by taking off their shoes at the entrance and proceeding barefoot onto the black and white marble of the salon.

Bisnonna appears on the balcony over the salon, unnoticed at first. But she makes herself heard right away, by banging the cane on the banister, bang bang bang. When Aunt Ada raises her eyes to the noise, Bisnonna waves the cane in the air and calls out, "About time you paid a visit, Daughter!"

Aunt Ada rushes up the stairs as fast as she can, ample breasts bobbing ahead; Rico follows at a respectful distance, smiling.

Weeks pass, and our visiting relatives are in no hurry to go home. These are still times when you come for a visit and stay for three years, should circumstances allow, and the Grandparents' home has enough rooms to host a mature couple who still insist in sharing one bed anyhow. Ada and Rico prove to be quite unobtrusive. Rico goes out "to the Café" in the morning and only shows up at home for meals; Aunt Ada has taken to sitting in the linen room with Agata in the afternoon, when Agata always reverts to her traditional ironing duties, after spending the morning in her new housekeeper's capacity.

The linen room, which I have always loved, takes on a new feel. The smell of clean linen dampened for ironing is still there, of course, but it no longer dominates the room. There's something new in the air. The linen room has only ever been part of the servants' quarters before La Signora's Sister chose to spend most of her afternoons there. She likes chatting away over her needlepoint while Agata irons. Gigi tells his wife that La Signora wouldn't possibly approve of such familiarity between house staff and their employers' family, but Agata points out that La Signora is not there to see it, and that La Signora's Sister, Mrs. Salvo, is half American by now and everybody knows that Americans are democratic. Anyone can see that in the movies.

There is a large armchair, straining at the seams, in the linen room. I sneak up to it in the afternoons and keep as quiet and still as possible, until Aunt Ada and Agata forget about my presence and start chatting again.

It's by sitting quietly in this armchair that I learn two things I will remember often, later. You don't mess with the women in my family. And, the women in my family would do well to give up fighting in favor of hugging, every once in a while.

"So that's how I met Rico," Aunt Ada says, "in church. There was no other place I could have met him; church was the only way to get out of the house except for Wednesday afternoons, when I did volunteer work at the Charity Hospital. That meant Rico wasn't going to get a chance to talk to me; Mother had already noticed that he was looking over at our pew most of the time during Mass every Sunday. She had noticed and she had asked about him and his situation in life – you know, did he have employment and what kind, did his parents own their home – the usual. She had asked our neighbor Mrs. Brosio, who knew everything about everybody in the neighborhood; Mrs. Brosio had taken a week for research and had come back with the news that Rico was, or wanted to be, "an inventor."

"A … what?"

"An inventor. One of those people who think up things that don't exist yet – say, the automatic potato peeler, before it was invented, or the radio – and then build them. And sell them. An inventor."

"An inventor wasn't good enough, because Mother had not been able to find news of anything that he had already invented around the neighborhood; much less of anything that he had actually been able to sell. So Mother walked across the church aisle the next Sunday, and told him clear and loud to keep his eyes off me; his courting was not welcome; she and her husband would not tell him again. Then she crossed the aisle back to our pew with everybody and the priest staring, and all the women whispering to their neighbors. And she also told me off, but not loud, rather hissing sideways in my direction; she told me to keep my eyes lowered and be sure to act proper, or else. Too bad, because I liked Rico and had started returning his smiles when Mother was not looking."

They work on in silence. Agata moves on from ironing sheets to taking care of the men's suits that have been waiting on their hangers all around the room, and have to be brushed with water and vinegar, before they can be aired on the balcony and ironed in turn. The smell of the room changes again, from fresh linen and cookies to fresh linen, cookies and French salad dressing. I like it even better. Halfway through the first pair of pants, Agata talks again.

"So how did you and Mr. Salvo get them to change their mind?"

Aunt Ada looks up from her needlepoint. "We didn't." Then she pauses again.

Agata hangs the pants near the window and takes the coat off the hanger; dips the brush in the vinegar and water.

"We didn't. After Mother's public show of disapproval it was totally out of the question that we would get away with seeing each other, in the neighborhood. That's why I joined the Red Cross ladies and made sure that everybody in the neighborhood knew."

Silence, again; unhurried. Agata is almost finished with the first suit, but has three more to go; Aunt Ada needs to switch from blue thread to red and takes her time choosing the right shade. She changes her mind a couple of times; goes back to her original choice and puts the thread through the needle, arms stretched out in front of her to bring it all in focus – she is no longer eighteen. But she has been; she surely has.

"That's also why Rico shot his own arm. And said that it had been an accident, of course."

Agata stops her brush on the cloth and looks up. "He shot his own arm ... ?"

"Yes, a leg would have been too private a part of a young man's body, they might have chosen to assign him an older nurse, even if there weren't many available at the time; you know, a married nurse. That's why he chose the arm; he had a much better chance of being assigned to a younger nurse – me, for example."

Agata wakes herself up, resuming the slow strokes of the clothes brush, but she still has her eyes wide on Aunt Ada's face. Aunt Ada is looking down at her work, comparing the new shade of red to the old. "Not quite dark enough."

Agata then slowly resumes her brushing. Silence, once more. And the smell of vinegar. And the clock on the wall ticking away heavily.

Then Agata just has to ask.

"And did he get assigned to you?"

"Sure he did."

I'm as curious as Agata, but I'm not about to speak — or even move, lest they remember I am there and Aunt Ada cuts out all the interesting parts.

"Did ..." Agata is not sure if she should speak already, "... did your parents change their mind when they saw that Mr. Salvo was wounded? And you took care of him? Or ... or when did they change their mind?"

"They didn't. I told you, they didn't. We had to do without them."

Agata lifts her brush from the clothes. "Without them?"

"Well, as long as we still could. My uncle was a priest — you may never have met him in this house, he died young; but he was a priest. He agreed to marry us in secret when I told him that I had lost my virginity to Rico. Not that it was true, of course. We just had him believe that, so that he would agree to marry us immediately. Then, we went back to our separate homes — to our parents. We would meet in the garage where Rico worked on his inventions; my parents thought I was going to the hospital, every day, for my volunteer work." She stops sewing and smiles at the embroidered cloth in her hands. "We should have known that it couldn't last that way of course."

She keeps smiling a while, hands and cloth resting in her lap. Agata has given up brushing altogether and stands holding her brush in mid-air, mouth slightly open.

"They found out that you weren't going to work?"

Aunt Ada looks up and laughs outright. "Oh, no, no, they never did! It's just that I became pregnant with Gina, and four months later it began to show! I had to tell Father the truth before he killed me or threw me out! I had to admit to being married, at that point ..." She really finds the recollection amusing. She shakes her head, still laughing some, and she says, "Oh, was I young then, I was so young."

I see Agata raise her eyes from Aunt Ada's happy face to the door. I turn my head very slowly and I see Gigi on the threshold. How long has he been there — an unperceived honorary member of this women's circle?

He is smiling, too. He shakes his head. Then pushes himself away from the door frame he's been leaning against with both hands, and walks off into the hall.

A few weeks later, I hear Bisnonna's story, in that same linen room where our very present past is being revived. It is the story of the family's migration from the poor region Abruzzi into the industrial North of Italy.

It didn't happen out of dire necessity, from a desperate hope to earn a decent living or even just the wish for a better life. It was for none of the usual reasons, at least not on my great-grandmother's part. Her husband, Nonno Costante, took off first. Alone.

Nonno Costante liked to sing 'the opera'. The whole village praised his voice; but it was to be heard in church only, of course, and only ever at weddings. Costante had memorized the tenor's part from all the operas that his much beloved Verdi had ever composed; Costante's mighty voice would be inviting Violetta to rejoice — "Brindiamo, brindiamo" across the village, down the Via Garibaldi, which ran from his house to the village square.

One day he finally announced that he was going to Milan, to sing at La Scala and make them all rich; he told his wife to pack for him and was off on foot — with his peasant's clothes pressed into a cardboard suitcase — to the train station in Teramo and to his glorious future as an internationally renowned performer.

Bisnonna Paolina only started to worry when she realized that she hadn't heard from him in three months. Not one postcard from the City of Singers, much less a letter to tell about his successes at La Scala, or inquire about his two little girls. Not that Paolina could actually have read the letter — she could neither read nor write; but Costante did know that she would have had Don Mario, the Vicar, read it for her — as everybody else in the village did when a letter came; and the next Sunday after Mass, everybody would have stopped outside the church to congratulate her and ask her what she would do with all the money that Costante the Famous Singer from La Scala was sure to start sending home now.

Paolina had to fend off comments and questions of a much less friendly nature when five months had passed; as the sixth month expired, she packed her own cardboard suitcase with her Sunday dress and two warm sweaters for the children. The three of them took off to the station in Beppe's cart on a Saturday, when he was travelling into town as usual to sell his goat's cheese at the local market.

The trip must have been a frightful experience of discomfort and even fear. Women did not travel alone across

Italy in 1910, much less with two young girls; still much less if they could not afford first class. And as Paolina exited Milan's Central Station she must have been hit hard by the explosion of noise and crowd that unexpectedly met her eyes and ears.

She didn't even look for a place to stay. She asked one policemen after another for directions to La Scala – the Vicar back at the village had said that the only strangers you could safely address in a city were the policemen, and to stay clear of all others, and not to answer if they spoke to you. She actually found the theatre – and, incredibly, she actually found her long-lost Costante there.

He was more seriously lost than expected. Paolina and the girls did not find him busy singing on stage – it was two o'clock in the afternoon, anyway – nor busy singing in general.

But busy he was, right then, with an opera star's personal maid who had been straightening out her mistress's dressing room. As it turned out later, Costante had access to La Scala, off hours, in his capacity of official (singing) handyman.

Paolina recovered from the shock faster than he. She sent him to the hospital with the mere help of a large umbrella she had been carrying, tied to her suitcase with a string. She had taken that umbrella with her from Abruzzi, as the Vicar had warned her that she might have to face very stormy weather, up North.

"Yes, Agata," Aunt Ada says. "To this day, as I'm sure you've noticed, my very old mother is perfectly ready to pick a fight, should she deem it necessary. People look at her and see an old woman who needs a walking stick just to stand. But we all know better, don't we? It's not three props; it's two legs and a weapon."

Little do I know that I am going to witness another show of my family's determination – when least expected.

Three years later, on a Monday afternoon, Gigi answers the doorbell and opens the door, as usual.

Grandmother stands on the threshold. She says, "Buongiorno Gigi." She doesn't even have a suitcase.

She takes one step into the entrance hall, and is back.

Pearls

No way can she be left alone to lunch today. Gigi summons Mother; Mother summons Father; and all are involved in a frantic discussion about who should tell Grandpa. Grandpa has his office in the next building, and will be home for lunch; he must be forewarned, lest a heart attack — or more likely one of his fits of anger — takes him away, now that his wife is back.

Grandmother has gone up to her room and is not to be seen.

She does show up for lunch, though; her place at the table has instantly opened up again, after all those mealtimes of slow but constant shrinking. Grandpa's place is also set; but Grandpa is not going to eat with us today. Father reached him at the office; he has come back saying only that Grandpa is to attend a business lunch and we are therefore not to wait for him; whatever has come to pass when Father made the incredible announcement is to remain between them.

When Grandmother descends to lunch, we are all standing behind our chairs in the dining room, dutifully waiting for the lady of the house to be seated. She appears at the door and looks around at each of us; then, to our great surprise, she smiles.

Once seated, she is silent, but the smile lingers on her face. Nobody else says a word either until Gigi comes in with the first course and stoops to lower the serving dish to an appropriate hovering altitude above the table.

"Oh, fettuccini, how lovely!" she says. She actually says "how lovely," and looks around as if inviting the rest of us to share in the pleasure of the fettuccini surprise.

That's when we all know that something is not, and will never again be, the same as it has always been before.

Grandmother passes through the following days without a sign of recognizing any alteration of the once-familiar status quo; with the preposterous exception of her new friendly disposition, not a word or act ever even alludes to the three-year "vacation". She doesn't hint at where she has been and what she has done in those three years; much less at the notion that she might owe an explanation to anybody, anywhere.

When Grandpa reappears, on the evening after her arrival, they are alone upstairs for a couple of hours, and only Grandmother shows up to dinner after that. She is pale but as incongruously friendly as she has been at lunch; she retires early but she actually thanks us for keeping her company; and she looks into the dining room, where the table is still being cleared, to say "Goodnight Gigi," on her way upstairs.

In a few days and after a few silent meals, Grandpa starts talking again, at least to us; in a couple of weeks we are excused from showing up every evening, and invited to visit again, "as always," for Sunday lunch. Much to their surprise, the Parents are also invited to a party to be held at the Grandparents' in three weeks.

"Grandpa and I want to celebrate my return home from vacation;" − Grandpa is silent and looking across the table away from his wife, and everybody else, "and I am very much looking forward to seeing my friends again, after so long. We will have a pianist of course, and we will make it black-tie." And then, "I think that young Carlotta should come too." My parents look at each other. "That is, only if her parents see it fit for her to do so. It could be seen as an opportunity for her to learn how to behave in the kind of situation she will find herself in more and more often in the future. I would be glad to provide the evening dress — anything you would consider appropriate for her age, of course" — to Mother.

Both my parents look at her blank-faced, too surprised to answer. Mother has never been openly recognized by Grandmother as the main authority on the children; Father, almost as little as his wife. Grandpa is still looking across the room and I — well, I am quite used to being spoken of as if I weren't there, but I have never expected to be invited to one of Grandmother's famous parties. Only my brother speaks up from the privilege of youngest age, "Are you now going to dance with Mr. Bertolotti, Sis, are you really?"

Not even Grandpa can stop himself from laughing.

One month later, the evening of the party has come. They all have pearls, the ladies. Either they are wearing them or they have them at home, you can tell. But most of them are wearing them tonight — two or three threads over shantung dresses that bare sleek shoulders and plump arms. Everything is round, about them, and they sit in twos and threes on sofas with rounded armrests; they hold their cigarettes in purple-nailed hands. The men stand, mostly in the immediate vicinity.

The French windows to the terrace are closed — maybe Gigi will open them later when people will dance, if ever they want to. Right now Gigi is busy carrying around the tray with the drinks. Agata is already standing behind the buffet in the dining room, her white embroidered apron over her black waitress dress. She wears white cotton gloves. The pianist is still choosing soft, off-hand melodies; he looks up into nothing, rather than face the pianist's wall in front of him.

And I stand on the threshold: between the servants' quarters, where Agata has helped me dress, and the salon, where Mother is attending to her duties with the guests and where everybody is in fact just waiting for Grandmother to appear at the top of the stairs, and walk down.

I am not so sure that I want to move from the threshold. Gigi is passing back and forth — full tray, empty tray — and smiling at me as he passes; but I know that in reality I am alone, this time. The French windows are still closed. The tall windows are way, way up high. And nobody has noticed me yet.

No. Mother has noticed me. She walks toward me with an encouraging smile. When she is upon me, she bends down to whisper in my ear. "You look pretty. We did choose the right dress. You look just right. Come, I will introduce you."

She takes my hand and draws me into the salon. I am wearing pale pink, with silver threads.

Mother walks my hand, with me attached to it, to the living room, where three women are sitting on two sofas next to one of the coffee tables. Once we are there, she waits for them to stop chatting and all turn towards us smiling; then she says, "Carlotta is with us tonight, for the first time."

"Oh, how thoroughly delightful! You have grown so much, Lotti, and you look so very pretty tonight! Beautiful dress," and to my mother, "from the Sisters Solange, I imagine?"

Mother nods and smiles.

"Oh, I could see that immediately. At the Sisters Solange one can always find something fully suitable for a young lady. Whether it is for an evening or just Tea. Yes, they also have the sweetest tailleurs for a young lady's afternoon."

The next lady nods her approval − "Quite so, quite so," and still nodding, now in a circle to all the ladies around the coffee table, "I don't go anywhere else anymore, for Loretta's clothes. The Sisters Solange are quite the thing, for young ladies."

I turn to the third lady on the next sofa, expecting her to repeat this thing about the Sisters Solange that everybody is supposed to say at least once. But no; the three of them seem to have exhausted their potential for comment, and have all turned to Mother with purple lips frozen in a single smile. I am terrified that Mother will leave me with them; but she signals differently by gently squeezing my hand, which she still has in hers, and turns towards the next group. I follow my hand and my Mother over to a group of standing men. They stop talking and immediately look in our direction, as if they knew that ladies are approaching and the nature of their conversation must change. One of them turns an enormously protruding belly our way, along with his head and a Martini glass.

"You already know Mr. Bertolotti quite well, don't you, Carlotta. And Giorgio, Edoardo, please meet my daughter Carlotta. She is with us tonight for the first time. Carlotta, this is Mr. Landi and Mr. Poletti."

Mmh ... Poletti? Father of the "crying lady"? The one I heard about at La Colombella, three years ago, when I was little and the Storm came? Is she here tonight, and if so, where is she? I slowly look around while mother is busy smiling at all the usual comments on "how-she-has-grown". But mother has now let go of my hand, even if she is still standing beside me, and I consider running. They are now addressing me directly; I stay.

"Nice to have you with us, young Carlotta, at long last. We have been hearing so much about you."

"And rightly so," Mr. Bertolotti says, "quite rightly so. The most beautiful hair at the party."

He raises his glass to my hair. The other men raise their glass also and smile at my hair — except one of them, whose head is already turned towards the salon door. Through the door, we see two ladies sitting in separate solitudes in the armchairs that flank the glass-top table in front of the fireplace.

Mother's eyes follow the man's for a moment, then she moves on. We now approach yet another group, still in the living room. Stiff Louis XIV chairs around yet another coffee table. Mother has not taken my hand again; she knows that I know, by now, that I am to follow.

"Oh, here she is, the young one, as promised. Let me see. Oh yes, you do look pretty! I had heard already, that you had grown so much. Quite a young lady, quite a young lady indeed. And such a pretty dress. Sisters Solange?"

Somebody calls Mother's attention; she turns and walks off — apparently confident that I can handle the Sisters Solange routine alone. That proves to be only part of what I have to handle now, though, as the next lady, who has stuck to the standard smile while scrutinizing me from behind her raised glass, picks up the inevitable subject — my performance at school.

"I hear that you are a great student. Read a lot of books." Pause. "Do you enjoy that? Studying, being among books?"

"Yes, Signora, I do." She doesn't seem pleased. Wrong answer. I had thought the truth would do. "Well, commendable, indeed." Pause, again. "Just don't overdo it. You will need to take care of other things, too. And, you know, it's never pleasant to have a young woman mingle in men's subjects — politics and the like. I hear that you read history books." She pauses, for the third time. A longer pause, as she is now openly looking me over. She plays some pensive rhythm with her purple fingernails on the glass — click, cli-click. "I believe in reading for fun, anyway," turns away from me and to the next lady, "don't you?"

What am I supposed to say to that — somebody save me. Thank God, Fun-Reading Lady suddenly decides she is finished with me. She turns to the lady next to her, and the three of them regroup over some whispered wisdom that they all share and enjoy. They giggle. I am left standing there and, after what seems to be an adequately long spell of embarrassment, I wander off as if I know where I am going.

This party doesn't glow from within as all the parties of the past seemed to glow when I spied on them from the top of the stairs. The parties from when I was officially a child and Grandmother had not yet been on vacation. I used to watch from the half-opened door between the salon and the servants' quarters, and Gigi would whisk by carrying trays and whispering, "Careful," when he passed me, so I wouldn't jolt with surprise at being caught spying and overthrow the hovering goodies. I loved to watch the light in the salon back then: so much gloss and so much glitter. Grandmother's diamonds shot out thin blue rays when she passed the lamps.

When will the fun start, at this party? Something magical just has to happen; this is my first party among the grownups. The fun must be somewhere here – or all these people would not have come.

Looking through the door and into the salon, I think I recognize one of the ladies sitting in the lonely-armchairs. Yes, I'm sure now. The lady's name is Donata; she's the one who is "legally separated" from her husband. That should explain why she always shows up alone – not just here, also at La Colombella Country Club throughout the summer. I have heard that her husband has "a new girlfriend." So – are they married, or not? Anyhow, she always shows up by herself and spends most of the evening alone, just like tonight. I also heard that she has a new man; she has moved in with him. I heard that when the grownups thought I was not listening.

("Her situation ... in her situation, you know, openly living with a man who isn't her husband ... when you have put yourself in that kind of a situation ... oh, you know what I mean.")

I start to move towards Donata's chair. But I perceive a sudden change in the mood of the whole party; a flutter of excited whispers followed by a gradual hush. Then, incredibly, total silence, except for the piano. Everybody is looking up, now, and so do I — to see Grandmother descending the stairs to the salon in her white silk dress, a gracious smile bestowed down upon all of us from her upturned chin.

For the first time, I think, quite clearly, that Grandmother is beautiful. She still looks like a very old lady — she must be nearing sixty, but for some reason she looks like a pleasant version of an old lady. Probably because she's keeping up this new habit of smiling — and not only at ladies she meets for bridge, or in church from pew to pew.

Grandmother completes her grand entrance: slowly down the stairs, past the landing where the pianist is now soft and uncertain, and into the now silent crowd of guests. By looking at her you would think she has not noticed the hush. She walks straight up to Mrs. Bertolotti; she looks unhurried, and she is still smiling.

"Adelia, how very kind of you to come."

Adelia Bertolotti blushes, glances quickly left and right, then she accepts Grandmother's arms loosely extended in front of her in an offer of the customary air kiss.

Grandmother turns to Mr. Bertolotti and offers her hand to be kissed. "Franco." Franco takes the hand and lowers his nose upon it, without touching, just as you are supposed to do it. Then he raises his eyes and — looking up from a still somewhat bowing stance — actually says, "It's lovely to see you back. I hope you enjoyed your vacation fully?"

Among the frozen onlookers, I can hear the sound of cracking ice.

Grandmother does not move; she does not retract her hand from what proves now to be Bertolotti's firm grip. She looks him straight in the eye and says, "Quite. A wonderful vacation indeed. You should take a vacation too, as soon as you get a chance. One feels so recharged, afterwards."

Bertolotti lets go of Grandmother's hand, but Grandmother does not let go of Bertolotti's eyes. Then, very slowly, she turns her head, and smiles at Grandpa. He stands stony-faced some three marble floor-slates away from his wife. She reaches him and puts her arm in his.

A few whispers surface from the crowd; slowly, normal conversation is restored among the guests. Even one actual laugh is clearly heard from the living room.

In half an hour, the noise of the party speaks for Grandmother's success. She has made it back and everything is back to what it always was, and "should always be."

I am not so convinced.

Something interesting has finally happened at this party: the ritual of the Comeback, through which Grandmother has returned to what was her world. And now I wonder if I am the only one who has noticed: Grandmother has walked up to the piano landing; she holds a glass of champagne in her hand. She offers it to the pianist, who hasn't seen her coming because he is sitting face to the wall. He looks startled. It takes him a few seconds to recover and accept the glass with a big smile, as she sets it down by the shiny black piano.

I wonder if I am the only one who has noticed, but of course I'm not. Gigi is still moving around in the salon with the tray, but very slowly, now; he is watching the scene for as long as he can without letting any guest go canapé-hungry. He also notices me watching. I look back at him, innocent-eyed; he holds my look for a moment before he lowers his eyes and smiles.

Now I'm tired. And bored. I have been introduced around, and I don't fit in any conversation here — nor would I be interested. And as for watching the goings-on — well, there's a limit to the time you can spend watching. And I have had enough of watching the tapestries — as I did when I was little, investigating details that repeated themselves hundreds of times along the walls of a room. The same gestures, the same phrases are repeating themselves along the walls of this party, carried safely from one group to the next.

It's not what I had expected. I walk out onto the terrace.

Alone in the free night air, I kick off my shoes, even though I know that I'll snag and ruin the first silk stockings I have ever worn in my life. I would like to kick off my stockings too, if one could kick them off; but no, you can only slide them delicately downwards after undoing those complicated garter hooks. I would never be able to hook them up again without Agata's help. Still, it's nice to feel the cool, uneven tiles of the terrace under my sole. I start dancing, on tiptoe, to the music that's wasted on the non-dancers inside.

"Hello." I hear, "Sorry, I didn't mean to startle you." It's Donata. I had thought I was alone on the terrace.

"Hello." I cross my feet one over the other in a little attempt at propriety.

Donata's chin points down at my unshoed feet. "That seems like a good idea." She smiles and takes off her shoes.

She dangles her feet from the bench she is sitting on, and swings her legs in rhythm. "Are you having fun?"

I need a second to decide if I am allowed the truth here. "Well ..."

"Yes. I agree. I know. It's always a letdown, the first time."

I breathe out. I've been taken by surprise. "But isn't a party supposed to be fun?"

Donata's smile shines back on me. "Yes. It's supposed to be fun. Sometimes it is. It depends on who you find at the party, or whom you invite." A pensive pause. "But the same goes for everything, I suppose."

I don't know how to respond to her; so I don't. Donata is now looking at the sky; I look too. No stars to be seen, too much light from the city, and from the party. But at least it's open space.

Donata snaps out of her contemplative spell and looks at me. "Nice dress. I recognize the style. I see that mothers still buy clothes for their girls at the same place they did when I was thirteen."

That couldn't be. This Donata woman must be at least twenty-five.

"Incredible" she mumbles. Then, louder — "Did you get to choose the dress? Mind you, it's a very pretty dress. It looks lovely on you."

"Thank you. No, Mother chose it for me." Donata nods and returns to her contemplation. I suddenly have to move because someone is coming out on the terrace through the door that I am leaning against. It's Grandmother. I jolt — caught without shoes.

But Grandmother says nothing; maybe she hasn't noticed. Believe it or not, she just smiles and looks up at the night sky. She puts a hand on my shoulder. She turns toward the bench and sees my barefoot accomplice.

"Good evening, Donata. I haven't had a chance to say hello to you yet."

"Good evening." Donata sits up but doesn't stand up — she is a grown-up with another grown-up, and a woman with another woman.

"Lots of guests to take care of, lots of people came," says Grandmother. She slowly walks over to the bench and sits down next to Donata. Donata looks just as surprised as I am. "Lots more people than I ever expected would come," Grandmother adds.

Donata turns her whole body towards Grandmother now, looks at her right in the face. Grandmother turns too, mirroring the other woman's movement; very, very slowly she starts smiling again — a curiously girlish look on her face. They sit for a few seconds like this, looking at each other. Then, they both turn to the wall in front of them and contemplate that.

I relax in their silence; I look around the almost empty terrace ... When my eyes go back to the bench, Grandmother is looking up at the sky. She says, "Too much light from this party. It makes it difficult to see the stars." She is dangling her feet from the bench and I see — I actually see that she has taken off her shoes.

Late in the season

Some ten days after the party I run into Grandmother on the balcony overlooking the salon. She has taken a chair and put it on the threshold to her room, facing in. She is seated, perfectly erect in the only way she knows how to sit. I walk by and slow down behind her. She's going: "Uhm..."

I say, "Yes, Grandmother?" more to avoid startling her than out of a belief she may have addressed me in particular. I don't expect her to explain that noise of hers. She does, however.

"What do you think of this room, Carlotta?"

"What do I think of your room?"

"Well, this room, yes. Is it a room that welcomes you in?"

"Me?"

"Anybody. Me too."

"Well ..."

"Speak up, young lady."

Speak up? That is something that Grandmother wouldn't have said to anybody, three years ago. Much less to a Young Lady.

"Well ... it's ... it's very full. To welcome someone in, I mean."

She nods, as if more to herself than to me. "Yes. That's it. Too full to let one in. Too full to let one think, also." Pause. "Now, why?" She's talking more to herself than to me.

My estimate is that no answer is required, as Grandmother seems gone with her thoughts, again. And I don't know what I should answer, anyhow. I learned long ago that is when you should shut up ... But then, lots of unprecedented things have happened in this home since Grandmother came back, and most of them were her doing.

"Maybe sometimes one does not want to think," I answer.

She turns to me in obvious surprise. She looks at me and seems to see me for the first time in years. Then she relaxes back in the chair and smiles. "Of course. Sometimes one doesn't want to think." Another pause. "I've lost track of some things. How old are you now?"

"Thirteen."

She nods. Then she turns her head slowly and looks at the room again for a while.

I look at the room too. I've always been fascinated by it — though, for some reason, uneasily so. This room is radically different from any other room in the house. All the others are furnished in elegant pre-war style: expensive Italian design of the thirties. Severe, linear, "modern".

Here, there's a lot of everything, and more; starting with the tapestry on the walls. The rest of the house is painted rigorously white-beige; in Grandmother's room, the same miniature pastoral scene repeats itself in china blue along the walls, and then drifts up to obsess the ceiling, too. Over the tapestry are flower paintings, and antique, mythical scenes. There are five different small table lamps in this room, and two *escritoires* with tiny locked drawers; plus the *toilette* where Grandmother hides the chocolate, of course. The bedspread reverts to dancing shepherds.

I come out of my spell before Grandmother; I wait a minute or so to see if she wants to say anything more. But she's still looking into the room from her uncomfortable seat across the threshold, her thoughts held in check by two fingers lightly set on her lips.

I tiptoe away.

Even I can see that Grandmother has had much more than a "vacation" in her three years away. Not that I have ever believed the vacation myth — it was of course one of those things that are made up once and repeated from then on.

All I have come up with so far is that Grandmother had grown tired of behaving, tired of Grandpa, tired of us all; she had possibly grown tired of feeling offended and angry, too. Maybe ... well, maybe she had taken a lover. That is quite a new idea of mine; I didn't think of it three years ago, when she disappeared. I have only come up with this fantasy recently — even though it does seem preposterous that a grandmother should take a lover.

I am sure, also, that Gigi knows more than anybody else. He was clear enough, back when Grandmother disappeared and I told him about the morning of the peach crostata in the Portofino hotel. Gigi was adamant that the matter was better left alone. I believe that Gigi usually knows what he is talking about, so I have "left it alone;" at least, officially.

However: something irreversible has happened to Grandmother. She now seems somewhat happier — but not only that; sometimes she actually seems "busy thinking," or looks as if she is actually listening to you.

Not that there is much to listen to. Grandpa is talking to her again, but only in public. If just family is there — we are not considered "public" — he fixes on the newspaper when she is in the room; at dinner, he talks to the fruit bowl on the table, and frowns his disapproval at it.

Grandmother appears not to resent this treatment particularly, or even notice it; she carries on a conversation with the back of the local-news page, or briefly enters Grandpa's field of vision by extending her arm to take an apple from the fruit-bowl he is addressing.

She has made good progress, anyway, from the original wall of silence; I can see that. It all started on the night of the party, when she took her husband's arm after facing up to that blob Bertolotti. A very quick flicker went through Grandpa's eyes that night, when his wife turned away from the society shark and took her husband's arm. I saw it. I am sure that I saw it; I was only uncertain if the flash was mere surprise or more admiration. Or was it just the recognition of a long-established common ground?

Sunday luncheon, almost as it used to be. I am not swinging my legs because I am almost fourteen now. My younger brother Alberto is wearing a coat and tie to Sunday lunch, now. But Grandmother has granted the men permission to take off the paraphernalia, given "this unpleasant heat."

The meal is almost over and Grandpa is eyeing the fruit bowl that has been placed at the center of the table, as always, for dessert. He is looking at it with resentful desire: as everybody knows, he loves fruit but hates to peel it so much that he sometimes skips it rather than pick up a knife and go through the trouble. Today his decision — fruit and peel or no peeling, no fruit — is going to be particularly difficult, as peaches have been served, and he has a thing for peaches. In the old times, when he was still officially speaking to Grandmother, he used to ask for them in June already. He would complain that Grandmother did not allow them until they stopped being *primizie* (a word charged with a sensuality that simple "early peaches" could never convey) and were then valued slightly cheaper than gold. But today they are there, with the hot weather. They are ripe and red and yellow; their fragrant velvet skin waiting to be shed — or slipped off like a perfumed gown, to reveal the juicy pulp that promises to fill your mouth, up to your brain and down to your heart.

The peaches are waiting in the fruit bowl in the middle of the table. Grandpa isn't touching them, at least not yet.

My brother Alberto takes one. Against all rules, he smells it and then gently rubs it against his cheek, smiling ecstatically, making soft noises of delight. Everybody else at the table looks at him, but nobody says a word until mother comes out of the general spell to say what she should: "Alberto put down that peach and eat it if you want it, or leave it on your plate if you don't."

Alberto complies — he puts down the peach but keeps trying to smell it surreptitiously with tellingly dilated nostrils.

Gigi has come to the end of his second round and is about to leave the dining room with the fruit bowl, when Grandpa raises his right index finger one inch from the tablecloth. Gigi notices — through that eye he keeps hidden on the back of his head — turns round and offers him the bowl. Grandpa takes his time considering all the peaches that are left, before he finally raises his hand to one, puts it in his plate and resumes his staring — at the peach on his plate, now. He still hates to peel that fruit.

Then, something happens. Grandmother looks at the peach, looks at Grandpa, looks at the peach again, and says:

"May I." No question mark.

She takes the peach, places it in her own dish and proceeds to peel it. Grandpa jolts at the sudden theft, but is too surprised to say a word. By the time he has regained his composure, Grandmother has peeled one quarter of the peach, and put it back on her husband's plate without looking at him. Now, he is staring for real — at the quarter fruit. Grandmother looks absorbed in peeling the second quarter of the peach. She is working at it slowly now — determinedly; she has a barely perceptible smile on her face, but it is unmistakably aimed at the peach on her plate.

Grandpa puts his knife and fork to the first peeled quarter, cuts it still in two, spears it, forks it into his mouth, and chews, looking straight in front, and not at any at us. We are so quiet. Grandmother is now peeling the last quarter — very, very slowly.

Young Alberto is the one who breaks the silence. He has been looking at Grandpa's face as if mesmerized. He now sighs audibly, "Mmmmh ... "

§

Things are mellowing with the season, and the sun now circles low enough to shed early afternoon rays through the dining room windows onto the table. It shines into my eyes when the whole family meets for Sunday gatherings, and makes Grandmother and Grandpa's backlit faces unclear.

Peaches have given way to figs, and then grapes, then apples. Grandpa now says "thank you" when Grandmother gives him his first peeled quarter of fruit. He is gradually reacquiring the gift of speech in front of his wife; sometimes he even briefly comments on the weather as he sits down to lunch, and on the dessert as he leaves the table for his afternoon nap.

All grown-ups spend the hour that follows lunch in the same way. Even Gigi is expected to take his afternoon nap, head resting on his folded arms on the kitchen table. His working afternoon starts only a few minutes before Grandpa shows up again downstairs in a fresh shirt, cufflinks in place, to be served coffee in his study and then leave for the office in a faint cloud of cologne. Grandmother stays in bed and "is not to be disturbed" for another half hour. I know how things are done because I am always expected at the Grandparents for lunch after school on Wednesday. That's the day of the week when my blessed French lessons with Grandmother used to take place. I was expected to take a nap when everybody did;

then, I would join Grandmother in the salon after coffee had been served to her there.

The Wednesday routine has been resumed as a matter of course the very first week after Grandmother came back from vacation; only the French lessons have been dropped. I am now taking French at school and can therefore be trusted to reach an acceptable level of fluency soon enough — the level required to answer properly when addressed in the language of "good society" ... I am grateful for the death of the French Ü, but I still hate the nap. It confines me in the gloomy guest room for two hours. I've tried to kill time by counting the cracks of light from the closed shutters. I have come over with non-recommended books and a flashlight hidden in my backpack from school; best of all, I have learned to leave my body in one place and move my soul to another — a key skill if you want to survive those long school mornings where they repeat the same information for the umpteenth time, in the belief that we are all thick — rather than bored to death, as we are.

Today my soul is called back to my body suddenly, back to the guest room and to the house. I have heard Grandmother's voice accompanying Grandpa's down the stairs to coffee in his study. In all the Wednesdays before the vacation, I had never seen Grandmother get up from her nap to see her husband to the door. I go to the door and open a crack to witness what I suspect could be unprecedented news. There she is, following Grandpa downstairs; smiling at his descending back. I retreat from the door, as I am afraid they may be able to see me once they come to the landing. But I make sure I can hear. And I hear Grandmother say, "Do you expect to be able to come home a little earlier, tonight?"

"Are we having guests?" Grandpa asks.

"No."

"No?"

"No. Carlotta is going home at five, and since Gigi is driving her I gave him and Agata the evening off." Grandfather stops on the landing, but just where I can see him without being seen. It is a few seconds before he turns to face his wife.

And it seems like a very long minute before I realize that I am not going to hear the answer I have been eavesdropping for. What I hear instead is their footsteps resuming their way down the stairs, and the house door closing.

When I dare to look again, Grandmother is back in the salon and strolling absent-mindedly to her chair — a slow gait and that faint smile still on her face.

"Carlotta, come upstairs! Please join me in my room." Grandmother is calling me from the stairs over the salon. She has heard the doorbell and seen Gigi open the door to let me in.

It has been two weeks since the day I eavesdropped on the Grandparents. It is also two weeks since I have seen either of them, as there was no Sunday Lunch at the Grandparents' last week, for the first time I can remember. Grandmother has also apologized for not being able to have me over for lunch on Wednesday — some commitment or other that she and

Grandpa had made with a friend whose husband was seriously ill.

"Carlotta, I want your opinion on something."

Twice, in such a short time? Twice asking fourteen-year-old me for my opinion? Grandmother?

I make my way up the stairs and reach the door to her room. Or ... is it? I stop dead on the threshold, and for a moment I wonder if I have got mixed up with the topography of my own Grandparents' home.

Grandmother's room smells faintly of wallpaper glue today. The pastoral scenes are gone from the walls; the new paper is simply off-white. Most of the furniture is gone, too, along with the objects that were sitting on it until last week: tiny crystal bottles of all shapes, Capodimonte china dolls, Grandmother's collection of silver powder boxes, most of the lamps. Only two very discrete *abat-jours*, left and right of the bed; they shed a warm light on a solid-color cream bedspread — silk. Twin armchairs by the window. That's it.

"I made room," Grandmother says.

Renovations

So much has happened lately. Things have moved on from the renovated room, slowly but surely: Grandmother and Grandpa are sleeping together in Grandmother's now welcoming room; they decided to sell their vacation home in the mountains and buy in Southern France, "where they know nobody and nobody knows them." On the hills reaching up to Grasse, no young housemaid's face could suddenly pass the window in the next villa and remind Grandmother of past injuries (or, worse, tempt Grandpa into future mischief).

Four years have now passed since Grandmother's return. Indeed, Grandpa is finally growing old; his eyes are now capable of a mellow look that they never knew in his ribald years; I often catch him smiling at his wife's back as she turns to leave the room.

Bisnonna has died, the ninety-four-year-old victim of a dancing accident; she fell, and broke her hipbone, while teaching young Alberto how to dance the mazurka. Not that Alberto cares to know how to dance the mazurka; he just found Bisnonna fun and so went for any activity she proposed.

Bisnonna has died after summoning me to her side once more. As in the past, what she needed to say was "important and urgent."

"Don't you forget now, Young One," she said. "We have already decided that you will never throw yourself away, and that is settled. You do remember, right?"

I said I did.

"Now, there is something else that I need you to do for me. And when I say that I need you to do it 'for me' I mean exactly what I say. Even though this is also in your interest, of course. Here it is: you don't throw yourself away and you watch your Grandmother. You watch your Grandmother, now."

I was confused. "Watch over her, you mean? Take care of her?" I asked.

Bisnonna surprised me with one of her old coarse laughs, not what you would ever expect from the lungs of a dying woman. "Take care of her? Take care of her! I never met one who could take better care of herself. Though I didn't actually 'meet' this one; I made her from scratch ... Which accounts for a lot. What I mean is watch her — learn. It will make your life easier, later."

"Watch and learn what?" I asked.

But she was tired and said our conversation was over. She had always loved an opportunity to throw a cryptic edict, but this time I felt she was not really making sense. I already had a notion that wisdom can sometimes border on delirium — more so when life is so closely bordering on death. I left it at that, even though Bisnonna's words seemed senseless to me. At the time.

§

So Bisnonna is gone; Aunt Ada and her husband have long returned to Florida and are writing less and less, except the postcards Aunt Ada sends regularly to Agata.

So much of Grandmother's world still survives, though — the Sunday Luncheons, the weekday afternoon naps. Those bridge tables where she sits with women she refers to by their last names. Even the new car mysteriously seems to keep up the old car's habit of breaking down on the way to Portofino. And all this apparent permanence is surprising, given the rapidly changing times in the world outside Grandmother's door.

Alberto and I are definitely more exposed to those outside changes than anyone else in the family. Alberto is in high school now, and I am a freshman in college. Not long ago I had to skip over the body of my dead Ancient History professor, in order to rush out of the classroom with all the others after we'd heard the shot. The body was lying across the threshold; the attacker nowhere to be seen. The note that had been left by his body called him 'a typical representative of a rotten establishment'.

I have just turned eighteen, and I cannot believe how everybody in the family wants to discuss what they still think of as "my future" with me. Very often I am faced with choices far more pressing than finding a proper husband. Recently I have had to consider, for example, how much I really wanted to exercise my right to vote in the Student Body Elections. Visiting the polls meant a long walk between two rows of people from very different political factions who would suddenly unite in their disapproval of bourgeois democracy and make their views public by spitting at anyone going to vote. More than once I have had to decide which was the best tree to rush for and duck behind, when bullets suddenly flew across the street and into the crowd.

What goes on outside the Grandparents' home is never acknowledged, much less discussed, within. I have learned to keep my mouth shut about my political opinions and activities, and to answer with just a demure smile when some visiting friend of Grandmother's asks me, "what do the Young think the World is coming to?" That same demure smile comes in handy when my interviewer concerns herself with my personal status: "How on earth can such a pretty young woman, from such a good family, not have a suitable young man in sight yet?"

Grandmother's world has survived virtually unscathed – and reassuringly boring – until now.

But now private sorrow has struck. Grandpa is seriously ill.

I am sitting downstairs in one of those armchairs that seemed so lonely when I was a child. I am afraid that grandpa is about to go. I am also thinking. His last days may be perhaps a little less painful than the doctor's diagnosis: only ten years ago he wouldn't have been able to count upon a companion for hard times. Grandmother carries on with him in the spirit of the new deal that was born between them after her return from that famous vacation. She seems totally, willingly devoted to lightening his last, difficult months.

The phone rings and I answer a man's voice asking for Grandmother. The Grandparents still have only one phone in the house, downstairs. I go to get Grandmother upstairs, where she is reading a book in the chair next to Grandpa's bed, her husband dozing under the spell of pain-relievers that are still illegal, and therefore only available to the rich. I go to get her upstairs and walk her back to the phone in the salon, not knowing yet that I am also walking her towards the next milestone in her life.

She is wearing grey flannel and a string of pearls around her neck. She now stands at the telephone, listening, not saying one word after "Hello." She is perfectly still; her face has turned the same pearly color as her necklace in the few seconds after she has picked up the receiver. I hesitate to leave: I am not really sure everything is all right. But then she speaks and says, with apparent effort, "This would be, of course, impossible." Only at this point, does she raise her eyes to my face, signifying that I should leave the room. She is trembling slightly.

As I make my way back upstairs, I feel as if I've witnessed something that will prove very significant, but I don't know whether for better or worse.

I open the door to Grandpa's bedroom and see that Gigi has taken Grandmother's place; rather than sitting on the chair next to the bed, though, he is standing in a corner, still holding the duster he has been using on the staircase banister. He is looking at Grandpa. He turns and smiles at me from his corner. I wait for Gigi to come to the bedroom door, where I am still standing, and let us both out, closing the door softly behind us. I put my hand on Gigi's arm and he turns to look at me, slightly surprised, sensing the urgency.

"The gentleman from the hotel in Portofino just called," I say. I speak very softly.

Gigi does not answer right away. He moves his eyes from my face to the floor, as if to take in the news as slowly as it oozes up from the marble slates. "Uhm," he says then. He looks at me briefly, then back at the floor before he finally rests his eyes upon my face and says, "I guess there are things that cannot go unexplained for much longer, aren't there?" He sighs — loudly. "Come to the garage after lunch. I will be working on the Alfa Romeo."

And I am now going to hear the story, after so many years.

Grandmother's three-year vacation wasn't the first "vacation" she had ever taken. When Grandpa and she were together on the Riviera, before her long absence from home, they were seldom actually together. Grandpa would take off for days in a row, officially on fishing trips on the yacht of friends. Nobody had ever been introduced to these friends, much less seen the yacht (allegedly at anchor in the nearby port of Varazze). Grandmother had stopped asking questions. Instead, she had taken to disappearing herself during Grandpa's absences. Even Gigi had not known where she went; she would only have him drive her to the railway station and dismiss him before a train ever appeared.

But when she had left home once and for all, and made it official with that letter to Grandpa, she had been in hiding from everybody but not from Gigi. Apparently, Grandmother trusted the odd alliance that she and Gigi had developed through all those years of playing their little power games. She had written to his wife Agata at their home address, letting her know where she was and stating that, "should she need Gigi for anything" from now on she would contact him at that address "for obvious reasons." She did not ask for secrecy nor recommend discretion; that was a given. Even Grandmother knew that some people enjoy relationships where one can take some things for granted.

Almost three years had passed by the time she did "need him for something," and summoned him to Nice. The city turned out to be her new home. Gigi had driven up an alley from a gate to a villa that seemed inordinately small for his vanished employer. He had entered the building from the rear door, as the usual brass target on the gate advised "home staff and delivery men" to do. The cook opened the door, and told him to wait in the kitchen; Gigi waited for half an hour until a maid appeared to say that La Signora would see him in the front parlor.

And there she was, a little thinner maybe, but otherwise unchanged. At first, also unchanged in her ways: she was half reclining on the brocade sofa and said, "Good morning, Gigi," as if she had dismissed him only the previous evening after he had served coffee. But then she actually looked in his direction to speak to him: Gigi almost turned round to see who was standing behind him. She hesitated only briefly before saying, "I hope Agata is in good health?" This was much more personal than at any time in almost twenty years of their acquaintance, and definitely the first time that she had ever enquired about Gigi's family. He was able to reply fast enough, however, and say, "My wife is in very good health, thank you, Signora," still standing, hat in one hand, driving gloves in the other to signal his readiness to drive off on command.

"Gigi, you shall drive me back to Milan tomorrow. We leave at nine. My maid — whom you haven't met of course, her name is Rosa — will have my luggage ready for you to take down to the car at eight forty-five. You shall not drive me home, of course. I will be staying at the Barlasco Hotel, for the time being." She paused. "Undisturbed." This last word meant, of course, without anybody knowing about it, at home or elsewhere.

Gigi kept his eyes on her face maybe a few seconds too long.

"Should I reserve a late dinner, for tomorrow night, Signora? And ..." he hesitated a second too long, "for how many?"

She kept her eyes on his face as she answered, "For one."

Gigi was going to find himself in an even more awkward position than that, before they left. That same evening, he was gathering La Signora's suitcases in the large dressing room adjoining the master bedroom. The maid would fill them early the next morning after La Signora had chosen her outfit for the trip and moved on to the tub for her morning bath. The door between the wardrobe room and the bedroom was open; La Signora e Il Signore stormed in one after another, noisily, obviously unaware that they had a witness to the quarrel they were having. Gigi couldn't move, at this point, without passing the open door. At the risk of making his presence known, he decided to freeze where he was.

"That is not what I am used to, Carlo," La Signora was saying at a slightly louder voice then discretion would have recommended, "nor what I would ever consider getting accustomed to. You knew what my life was like before I left everything for you."

"We have already discussed that, haven't we, Elisa? Even before it came to this. I never let you wish for anything without giving it to you right away, if I can remotely afford it. Materially and otherwise. Or do you now deny that, also?"

"I did not give up my life to be 'materially' pampered, thank you. You know perfectly well that I had plenty of that, before I decided to leave it all for you. Dearly hoping, at the time, that I wouldn't have to regret it later. You know what I was hoping for, when I left ..." She paused, as if hesitating to deal the blow, "I was hoping for a real man."

Gigi was now as good as paralyzed in his corner. He had realized that the mirror of La Signora's toilette was reflecting Signor Carlo's dead-pale face and pursed lips for Gigi to plainly see — this meant that Signor Carlo would see him the minute he paid attention to that mirror. Gigi flattened himself against the wall, frantically asking himself how to find an inconspicuous way out. Luckily for him, the quarrelers were in too deep to notice anything else.

"I'm not talking about 'the material', as you call it," she was saying, "I am talking about having a man who knows how to take care of his woman. Who can show that he sees it as a privilege to be with her. Who wants to be with her at all times, rather than with anybody else. But you're gone every time you get a chance – now you think you have me – with stupid excuses. You are just like ... I should have known better."

Carlo was visibly trembling, his fists clenched. "If you think that's what 'a real man' is, if all you want is a reflection of your arrogant self, if what you want is a slave – then you are quite right. I am not the man for you." Pause. "You know what? Maybe what you really need is your old friend Gigi 'from your previous life'." And, incredibly, "Maybe you should consider him."

Behind the door, invisible Gigi stood in a cold sweat. But he was quick to duck as the bottle of perfume that La Signora had picked up and thrown in Il Signore's direction flew past its target and into the dressing room, over the silent witness's head.

So, now I know also that Grandmother lived in Milan for a few months before she appeared at the door of her old home one morning. Indeed, she then lived alone for the first time in her life, as only happens to widows, in her generation. She has "widowed" herself twice. She may have had the time to ask herself what it was that killed her relationships.

Grandmother is not coming down to lunch. I am reminded of the days when she would retire to her room and pretend to go without food or drink, eating hidden chocolate, to make her husband feel guilty enough to apologize. But now it is quite another story. It is obvious to me that she wants to be alone to think, remember and feel, after the phone call. I see that I'm taking for granted that she is not the same woman she was years ago.

After two days, having divided her time between Grandpa's bedside and her room, she comes down the stairs in the afternoon, dressed to go out in a navy blue dress and small blue hat, white pearls around her neck. Her pace is as slow and determined as when she descended the same stairs on the night of that party after her return.

Once more, I notice that she is moving to a different inner rhythm: her gravity seems lighter; her poise, unaware.

I have been in the salon, studying and waiting for my turn to move upstairs and take my place at Grandpa's bedside. I do this twice a week, to give Grandmother a chance to rest. When she reaches the bottom of the stairs she stops, looking at me for a moment before she actually seems to see me; then, suddenly, she smiles at me. After another short hesitation, she walks over and kisses me on the forehead. This is the first time she has ever done anything like that. Then she turns and heads for the door.

She will leave like that every afternoon, at the same time, for the next year, and be back at the same time, ready to take her place at Grandpa's side.

He dies one spring day, after asking her to please open the window.

Pendulum

At Grandpa's funeral the church smells of incense and pain and regret as churches sometimes do – a bouquet deprived of hope and celebration. Even weddings cannot clear it away for good.

Outside, it rains heavily. The so-called friends of a lifetime walk up to Grandmother and wait in line for their turn to touch cheeks with her in a kiss that won't ruin anybody's make-up. Then they go over to my father, whom they have known as a toddler, to place their painted fingernails on his shoulders in yet one more air kiss.

I am almost surprised to see all that pain on my father's face. It seems to me that he has lost someone he has never really had anyway, someone he has never known that well. Father grew up in a confessional boarding school, where he was sent when his pregnant mother declared that two children in the house was too many and would disrupt any attempt at civilized living. He left that school to join the navy and then married very soon after the war and prison camp. I don't expect that Grandpa taught him soccer, or ever took a walk with him alone on those mountains where they've spent a three-month vacation every year. But Father looks fixedly ahead, clenched jaw, feet slightly apart – and I am in pain for him, even though I do not quite understand why.

As the string of giant overjewelled black ants dribbles out of the church, I am distracted by sounds of a political rally in the next street, just outside the cemetery. It soon becomes so loud that it drowns out the bells tolling deep and slow.

One tall man in a dark-grey suit stands at the churchyard gates, face indistinguishable under a black umbrella. Alone and motionless, he looks at the small crowd to which he doesn't belong. He is witnessing the passing of a man whose life he has never officially touched. He is watching Grandmother perform her last duty to that man with obvious devotion, as if she knew, now, that some things should be done utterly well, or not done at all.

Three months after Grandpa's funeral we are in the salon, Grandmother and I, sitting in the same armchairs in which I was blessed with boring French lessons as a child. No French lesson now. Grandmother has been silent for a while, staring at the unused fireplace in front of her chair; lost in thought. I retain the old habit of not speaking first — even though that has ceased to be a requirement long ago. When in Grandmother's home, I just automatically still conform to the rules of the house from years ago. Some things have never changed: the smell of leather from the armchairs, the angle of the light from the tall windows around four o'clock in spring, the pendulum clock sounding toc, toc, toc. That clock still surreptitiously leads me, whenever I sit nearby, into counting how many tocs fit into one breath – in, out.

She says, "How old are you now? Eighteen, right, more or less?"

"Yes. Well, almost nineteen, actually."

Grandmother smiles. "That's over two years older than my mother was when she got married. When my parents got married, I mean." Pause. "Something tells me that you are not thinking of it yet."

I shake my head and add nothing. That is a subject I have learned to expect people her age to bring up with me. Grandmother's friends started bringing it up when I was barely sixteen. But she isn't going to pursue it, this time.

"I wish I had loved your grandfather, when I married him. I wish I had known better."

This is so personal, so unprecedented, that I cannot possibly have an answer. I raise my eyes to her face, keep silent and wait.

"All those years all alone," she says, "married to his money. All alone." She looks at the expression on my face, smiles again and turns her hands palm up on the armrests, as if to wave away my shock. "I don't mean that I minded the money, of course. I just wish that I hadn't settled for that alone. But then," her voice is small, lost inside of her, "I didn't know about anything else. I thought ..." She doesn't finish the sentence. She seems to come back to the room instead. She keeps her eyes on the tall windows of the salon, for a while. "Never figured out how to have those properly washed." Then she looks at the pendulum clock, the French windows to the terrace, the stairs leading to where the piano once was. "Have I told you yet, that I intend to leave this home?"

Of course, she hasn't. I am in shock, again – but now to the point of speaking. "Leave ... home?"

"No. Leave *this* home."

I can't recover from my surprise that quickly. It has never even dawned on me that someday, somehow, Grandmother would leave the house with the tall windows, and take the past somewhere else. She has left once before, of course, but she had left the past where it belonged that time, and had come back to it later.

"But ..."

"Things change, right?" She looks around the room again. "This is the home of another person."

That's true. But this has also been my part-time home, so to speak, for a number of years ... I have always found it too silent and suffocating; I have hated the conventions that regulated it – the conventions to which I have faked conformity. Could I have also loved it? Or been used to it? Do I still need the sound of Bisnonna's walking stick upstairs? The sound of Gigi banging the door once more, as he walks out to the garage? Do I still need Agata in the linen room, and the aroma of starch floating along with Aunt Ada's voice as she reveals the pasts of women who have come before me?

"I shall be sharing a home with Carlo, in Southern France."

Oh, Lord. "Carlo," she has said. "Carlo," as if she expected me to know who she is talking about. Carlo the unmentionable, and so far unmentioned – except very recently, as 'Signor Carlo', in Gigi's sad tale of ending love. It takes me a moment to find a non-committal remark to make. "Southern France?"

"Oh no, not to the same place where your Grandfather and I spent our summers in recent ... in the happy years. Still Southern France, but a different place – another happy place, I hope." She keeps her eyes on my face for a few more seconds, her head tilting to one side as if she were seeking a different perspective; then she looks down at her painted fingernails and examines them one after another, clearly without seeing them. "Carlo has been in Milan for the last few months. But I expect that you know about that also, already. What you can't know is that he moved here as soon as he heard about your Grandfather's illness. Not on my request, of course. We had no contact for the three months before I came home. He moved here before he ever knew whether I would let him see me, let alone be near me. And he has been waiting for me at the same place at three o'clock every day since I gave in after his phone call, and agreed to see him for what I thought would be a repeated goodbye – our last one, now that I had ..." she smiles and looks at her nails again, "... fallen in love with my husband. And was losing that same husband, whom I had found so late. And I was sad, and remorseful and tired and lonely. And far from the mood that you need for ..." another smile, "... illicit lovers."

She looks at the tall windows again, as if she could actually see something out of them, something other than a clueless sky. "As it turned out, though, Carlo had no expectations of a lover's role; he was actually here just to support me through hard times. Nothing asked other than an opportunity to do so – two hours a day. Talking. Walking sometimes. Places where we did not expect to be spotted immediately by the old crowd, of course."

Now, if she is referring to the Bertolotti and friends, that is by now a very old crowd indeed. Old in years, and also much older than Grandmother in their outlook on the world, or so it seems to me this afternoon. As for Grandmother and Carlo being spotted and wildly gossiped about: of course she could have counted upon that. Even those "loving" friends who seem to have forgiven her vacation, and never refer to it, still hold on to something, deep down, that they can never forgive: the lack of consequences. Not only has Grandmother worked her way back into society in spite of her sins, she has also worked her way back into her husband's favor. She has failed to pay the expected, due price for free choice. Her friends deem this unfair.

"He promised that if I let him be by my side through hardship, he would be ready to accept a dismissal, should it come to that, when my ordeal was over. Later, the day came when I told Carlo what my 'ordeal' really was: more than just accompanying a dying husband; it was about facing the loss of the man I loved. Other than Carlo. Carlo took it without faltering. Now I wonder if he already knew, then, what I still didn't: I was losing one of the men I had loved. And one of the two men who had loved me."

She is looking at the empty fireplace again. "See, it's hard to explain. One can actually learn from one man how to love another. How to let him love you, also. I know that, now."

As surprised as I am, at first, that Grandmother is talking to me like this, my muscles gradually relax into the armchair as her thoughts seep into me.

She repeats, "I know now. I had not understood." Then, a very long pause. The afternoon light is fading through those windows that are so large, and so tall, and always reserve the best of the day's glory for the later hours.

"Now I am going to finish what I started. And I will try to do it well."

This is my first and last real conversation with Grandmother. Before she leaves, she asks of me, as a big personal favor, that I take care of "giving away" the house. She is not going to sell it, after all; instead, she has almost agreed to let it to some people who have negotiated permission for a thorough makeover; the old house will still be there, but with no sign of the past it has contained.

I accept the task, of course, but I have trouble letting go.

Not so Grandmother, apparently; she has practiced letting go in life, and she is probably convinced, by now, that you can always go back to what you have genuinely owned.

The morning she leaves, she gives me a chance to own another piece of her life. I go up to her room to draw the blinds and find another letter on the bed.

After so many years ...

It is addressed to me, this time.

Letters

Dear Carlotta,

Only very late in life have I realized how it could be, that other people made choices so different from mine. Or why they seemed to question my motives for doing and saying what I said and did. But then, only very late in life was I exposed to a world other than the one I was born in or the one I had joined through marriage. Before I had ever lived outside the home of my father or husband, I had not known, nor enquired, if a different way of looking at things existed.

I am now convinced that if I had, earlier in life, I would have arrived where I am now at a lower price, for myself and for others.

That is why I am writing to you now.

There is a part of my past that you have witnessed, albeit through the eyes of a child; there is another part that you know nothing about – that you are probably too young to picture for yourself.

I have gone over my diaries and found a few passages that explain a lot. Namely, how I made a number of significant decisions in my life, based upon a somewhat skewed perception of what was happening. I am thinking, in particular, of a few seemingly unimportant episodes from those three years with Carlo – my so-called vacation.

Now I see such episodes as potential turning points ... at the time, I missed them and that cost me dearly; later I recognized them, and that saved me.

I am attaching an account of these episodes; I do remember quite vividly, even though I write as the woman I am now. If you look at the pages that follow, and remember what you witnessed yourself afterwards, maybe at some point in the future you will remember to question assumptions, especially when they make you unhappy or afraid. I do believe that that can sometimes save our lives – or, at least, a few of the remaining lives we have.

Your Grandmother,
Elisa.

Looking back at February 1964

Carlo and I were almost settled in our new home. He more so than me. I had had some trouble recruiting the household staff that I was used to and thought of as necessary. Carlo maintained that we had no need of a driver; he joked about my having to do without a lady's maid, for a while. He said that having to lay out my clothes for myself every morning would give me something interesting to do until lunch. As for himself, he seemed perfectly happy driving the car himself, working on its engine when necessary and even doing small repairs around the house. He brought me flowers but refused to change for dinner unless his clothes were dirty.

I was uneasy with his disregard for conventions; I would have been downright embarrassed, had we had more company than we did at the time. The family I originally came from had known nothing of "extravagant living". In the past I had regarded their attitude as belonging to a social class that I had wanted to leave — so much that I had been ready to marry a man, your grandfather, whom I didn't love.

What had started to worry me even more, was the fear that Carlo's relaxed attitude might indicate diminished respect for me, now that I had left everything to be with him. I told myself now that maybe I should not have dismissed the first signs as lightly as I had; I might have known from our first morning together ...

He had left my room at dawn and was now joining me for breakfast on the terrace of the hotel. We had agreed that he would show up some fifteen minutes after me and appear to be invited to join me at my table as a matter of politeness. He would be merely a casual acquaintance from the previous day. I extended my hand as he came to stand by the table and, unbelievably, rather than take it to his lips he shook it vigorously and said, "Nice to meet you," before opening up in a large rascal's smile. Thank God, I thought, he has his back turned to the other tables, so that nobody can have witnessed his untimely display of humor.

I had not enjoyed the joke. For a moment, I had asked myself if my lapse of the previous night had not compromised his respect of me, and if he would now fancy that he could address me, at any time, from the stance of an old friend — rather than how I wanted him to: as a grateful, humble admirer.

Looking back at August 1964

The season had brought some social engagements and I was grateful for them. In my old life in Milan, a lot of my time and thought had gone into maintaining contact with people I thought I didn't care for. For some reason, now I missed their company sometimes. Or maybe I missed the illusion of company ... or a reason to wear a new hat, as Carlo didn't seem to notice how I dressed. Or he didn't care.

There had been a concert at a fashionable place called Le Pavillon aux Roses, followed by a party at the house of a distant cousin of Carlo's, who always spent the summer in his villa further down the coast.

I had looked forward to that party as if it had been a new and unknown form of diversion, even though gatherings of that kind had been so frequent in Milan — with the same people all the time, come to think of it.

This time I was nervous. Carlo's cousin knew our story, and I expected everybody else to know as a consequence. The world had been changing fast in recent times; only a few years back we would never have been received ... But I could still imagine myself accidentally walking in on a group gossiping about our presence in town ... I had come up with all sorts of worries, in view of that party. I mentioned it to Carlo, one night; at first, I thought that I had made a mistake in doing so.

"Well," he had said, lowering the paper that he had been reading, "I had always thought of you as a very self-assured lady." He was smiling; but I already wished that I had said nothing. My mother's old words flashed into my mind immediately: "When a man is no longer afraid to lose you and changes his mind about any trait in your character, it is usually not for the better." I panicked, even if I knew better than to show it. Carlo went on, "How would our story be any of their business? And even if it were, or if they made it their business because they have nothing more interesting to busy themselves with ..." He lowered his eyes to the newspaper, as if ready to pick it up again. But he didn't; he looked at me again, and again he smiled. "You know, Elisa, I have sometimes thought that people enjoy punishing you for living as they don't dare. But they only try when they think you are vulnerable. They try to punish you when you look punishable, when you somehow show that you are open to it. Sharks are blind, you know; they attack when they can smell the blood." He was looking at me straight in the face; he was absolutely serious. Then, he picked up the paper again.

I fretted my days and nights away until the evening of the party. And, incredibly now, I was angry with Carlo. I felt abandoned, left to deal with the approaching social ordeal on my own resources alone. As if he hadn't been responsible for our situation as much as I was, I told myself. As if I hadn't had much more to lose, when I had followed him, than he had had by taking me away.

I ended up doing rather well at the party, after all. Carlo thought so too. As we were on our way home and he was about to start the car, he turned to me and said, very slowly, "You were absolutely great." He then kept his eyes on me for what seemed like a long moment of outright admiration. And desire.

The next morning I woke up to a feeling of warmth — but that didn't last. With my morning coffee, my nerves were on edge; by the time I was ready to go out, I knew the source of my fretting. I didn't feel secure, not yet. The previous evening I had succeeded — I had kept my head high enough for nobody to dare; but I had done it on my own. With his support and advice, but still on my own. And I wondered what would have happened had I not been up to it. Would he have let me go under alone? Would he have floated away on a sea of complacency? He was still socially acceptable; he had received ready forgiveness for his "crime of passion". That's what he could expect, of course, as a man.

Looking back at our first rainy April

Carlo liked to watch the rain. The first time I found him sitting alone in front of the tall window in the parlor, he had opened the panes and was looking outside with his back to the door. I looked outside from behind him: nothing interesting to be seen; it had been raining for three days in a row and the view was still the same wet hills dripping down into the sea.

Carlo had not heard me step in; when he felt my presence, he turned towards me with one of his smiles — one of those smiles that make other women crazy. Once more I thought that he looked so much younger when he smiled. He looked as if he had suddenly turned much younger than me. Too young for me, maybe.

"What are you doing? I asked.

"Watching the rain."

"Oh. And why do you watch the rain?"

"I just love to see it coming down so evenly. So patiently. I don't enjoy a storm half as much." And then, "You mean that you never watch the rain? I have never seen you do that, actually ..." The dangerously charming smile was still there ...

No, I did not usually watch the rain. I might have done so as a child, but I did not remember doing it, or ever seeing someone do it as a grownup. The grownups in my head would have said, "What do you accomplish, by watching the rain?" The women in my head were saying now, "He expects you to share his strange taste for wet days, and has a right to."

I had to answer Carlo, at this point; I lied. "Sometimes."

"Let me pull up a chair for you." He stood up.

I couldn't think of anything but, "It's almost four. Shouldn't we be having coffee now?" But he already had a second chair next to his by the window, both chairs facing outwards as if we were at the theatre. He held out his hand to me. "Come, let's watch the rain together."

So I sat and watched the rain. I really tried to find it somehow interesting, as Carlo seemed to, but I really couldn't. I grew bored, and didn't dare to say so. I looked at Carlo, only turning my eyes in his direction, my head perfectly still for fear that he might notice.

And then I felt it, and it was the first time. I don't know if it was in his profile, or if it flowed through the hand that was holding mine: I suddenly perceived an intensity, in him, that I found disquieting – a concentration, fiery and quiet, on something that transcended the drops of rain on the window pane and even transcended the two of us, in spite of our closeness.

Whatever it was, it was too much; I didn't like it. I pretended I had heard the doorbell and took the opportunity of Rosa's being out on her free afternoon to mutter something about seeing who was at the door.

I let go of Carlo's hand.

Opening

Three weeks after Grandmother's departure, the doorbell rings – yet another house-viewer. I am accepting more appointments than is probably strictly necessary, but I want to give the old house a better chance than the redecorating tenants Grandmother is ready to take in.

I beat Gigi to the door. It is getting increasingly easy to do that, even though he always tries his best, seeing it as improper that I should open the door myself. He stops halfway to it, this time, seeing that I am already there. But he gives me the usual disapproving look for when I win the race, before he turns back towards the kitchen.

I open the door and my eleven o'clock is slouching against the jamb, looking up at the entrance ceiling. He stands up straight as if caught in blatant impropriety and manages to say, "Buongiorno signora," from an unexceptionable posture. I answer, "Buongiorno," and add the name I have been given on the phone, half checking and half greeting.

He walks in and takes a quick look at the large mirror in the hall, then once more at the ceiling, but his eyes keep coming back to me. He must have noticed that I have noticed, because he smiles apologetically and says, "I had expected ... you know ... an older lady ... The person I talked to on the phone said that the owner was letting the house as she was retiring away from the city."

I smile back. "That is so, actually. The retiring lady is my grandmother."

"Oh." He rests his eyes on me for a second longer and then turns to look towards the salon. I walk into it ahead of him.

This man really must have a thing for ceilings, I tell myself; he is looking up again. He opens up in a wide smile as he notices that a ceiling is completely missing, so to speak, here in the salon; at least, between the two floors. He turns to me, "Beautiful space. And there must be a terrace, there." He walks towards it. "I like how the whole room seems to lead up to it." He looks upwards again and murmurs, as to himself, "Or up to those windows ..."

Stranger man than most who ever walked into this room, I think. And the first person who ever mentioned to me that the room leads you upwards, and out. This has always been quite obvious to me – though to me only, I thought, until now.

We walk into the dining room, and then into the sitting room, which he appreciates for being so bright and "large enough to accommodate instruments."

"Instruments?"

He turns to me with his entire body and smiles more broadly than he has done so far. "Musical instruments. A very large Bechstein, in particular. I like to practice in a large room. I like it when the boys come in to sit and listen. Soon enough they may be able to join in, when I am at home and playing for fun. It's a little scene I enjoy dreaming of."

"The boys. How old are they?"

"Oh, still very young, my oldest is eight, the others follow closely ... Three of them." Another broad smile. "That's why I need a large house. Three boys plus the nanny. Plus me of course. Plus some house help if I can find it — la Signora Giacometti has enough on her hands with the boys, when I am not with them. She has been with us forever now, one way or another; she can't be expected to run after the children as she used to."

I think of Gigi. As our visitor and I walk back into the salon, I see Gigi standing in the doorway from the pantry. He looks at me, then at our guest, then at me again. "Should I show the gentleman upstairs?" Obviously not a question. He is saying that there is no way I shall go upstairs alone with a perfect stranger. What do we know about this man? If he wants to go upstairs then he, Gigi, is going to have to be there too, on some excuse or other. We start up the old granite stairs as a party of three.

We reach the door to Grandmother's room; our visitor says, "Nice. I like the light, and all this white." The phone rings downstairs.

I am on the phone longer than I want. The caller is — no less — the Bertolotti. When she realizes it's me on the phone her voice drops the sharp edge — something she obviously hasn't deemed necessary when she thought that a 'servant' was at the other end. That is in itself already irritating enough, without having to ward off the usual nosy questions on what I think of my grandmother's decision to leave the city "again", and am I getting engaged yet ... ?

It must be ten minutes before I am able to hang up, and the two men have obviously continued their visit upstairs, in the meantime. I decide to wait for them downstairs and I drop into one of the armchairs by the coffee table. Funny, I don't hear the men's voices any more ... What I hear instead, to my surprise, is a knocking sound come from above, way up. I turn to the balcony that overlooks the salon; there is nobody there. The knocks come again, and my eyes then follow the noise to the tall windows.

There they are. Gigi and the visitor are looking in from outside one of the windows, waving and laughing, looking much like a pair of suspended puppets.

The sight defies reason. Those are the famous unreachable windows that my Grandmother complained about never being properly cleaned. The very same windows that have so long denied me a view of the outside, except for the flocks of swallows against a blue backdrop.

My large puppets are now working at something on the outer window frame, until I hear a clank and the panes dislodge towards the inside. I scream and put my arms over my head, expecting the panes to crash down into the salon and drag the two men along into the chasm below.

Incredibly, nothing happens. When I look again, the windowpanes are still hanging there, simply opened onto the salon from above.

The two men are cheering. "We opened them, Miss Lotti, they can be opened!"

Our visitor looks at Gigi, and then at me, in amusement. "Hadn't anyone really ever noticed the outside lock, here on the balcony?"

I don't have an answer. I am still recovering from the shock of seeing two men hover in space and then escape the inevitable ten-meter drop. It takes me a while to comprehend the obvious existence of an upstairs balcony that I have grown up ignoring. There must be a door onto the ghost balcony, upstairs; have I possibly never seen it? Never gone by it? Grandmother's is a very large house, but children are natural explorers of out-of-the-way possibilities ...

The ghost balcony places the tall windows within reach; it has always placed them within reach. It would have been enough to go upstairs, step outside and have a look at things from ... well, from outside, which often makes for an unexpected angle.

I remain sitting in the chair. The two men reappear on top of the stairs, still laughing. Gigi is talking to the Stranger now in a relaxed tone that I have only heard him use with my father, years ago. "Had it not been for you, Sir, those windows would have stayed closed forever. We had never even looked for that lock! Thank you, Sir."

My tenant-elect answers in mock solemnity. "Guess that was our calling, then, Signor Gigi. Guess we were the ones meant to finally open those windows; and the day was today." He turns and leans over the banister to smile at me. I am still sitting in my armchair in the salon. He chuckles. Then he lets the chuckle go so that only his smile remains. There is a very quiet look, at me, before he starts down the stairs.

Thanks

I would like to thank all those who enjoyed my stories, told me so, and encouraged me to publish.

My friends of long ago, who used to say, Why-don't-you-write-this.

The later friends who took the time to read the first draft of this book and showed enough guts to give me feedback.

My invaluable editor, who never settled for less than good and managed to make me laugh on the way.

And of course Matte, who believed in me much before I did myself.

Luisa Brenta, Berlin, May 2014

About the author

Luisa Brenta used to spend most of her time helping others to write as part of their profession. Now she writes herself, as part of her life. Her work has appeared in literary magazines both traditional and online.

She was born in Rome; after much travelling she is now happily settled in Berlin. But, of course, she still remembers the blinding light of the South.

The Company of Men is her first book.

Other books from Pure Slush

For the complete range of *Pure Slush*
books and eBooks, fiction and non-fiction,
visit the *Pure Slush Store* at
http://pureslush.webs.com/store.htm

itch
by Gary Percesepe
ISBN: 978-1-925101-21-8
Originally published November 2013

Gary Percesepe writes beautiful, vivid stories with the intensity and brevity of a man on the run. His fiction lights up the page with incredible bursts of poetry, passion, and pain channeled through characters whose names we rarely catch. In just a few short pages, Percesepe captures entire worlds of emotion – all of it so true and real, it's impossible to look away.

Jessica Anya Blau

itch is a shrewd, swift-moving collection about urges, obsessions, and the energy of desire. Gary Percesepe's stories work together to expose and examine a curious cycle – the way our reality drives our fantasies and our fantasies influence our reality.

Jen Knox

Gary Percesepe drops you into an ambiguous world and pulls you back again, still reeling. He does it so deftly, you don't even realize you're bleeding until it's over.

Heather Cox, author of *California King*

falling and other poems
by Gary Percesepe

ISBN: 978-1-925101-24-9
Originally published November 2013

Percesepe's poetry seems straightforward but is as complex as flowers, as summer shade and layers of snowfall, available to all but folded around secrets only broken lovers or philosophers grasp, and contained by no borrowed forms but original truths and no meter but the throbs of a heart. He here assays breakfast making and love making and loss and memory and time and husbands and wives and offspring and always, always, the elegance of the line, the object plain or sublime or both, the landscapes of sex, sorrow and high style.

James Robison

The Merrill Diaries
by Susan Tepper

ISBN: 978-0-9922778-2-6
Originally published July 2013

The Merrill Diaries follows a quirky young woman running from a couple of doozy marriages but mainly from herself. Humor as well as pathos are discovered as our narrator opens up to the world, takes risks, and learns. The language is whip smart, the characters live and breathe on the page. A beautiful book.

Bonnie ZoBell

The Merrill Diaries takes you on a wild ride you don't want to exit. This novel in stories is the end of innocence and the start of "the broken tracks, the roads where the river has flooded over."

Gloria Mindock

Hard
by Dusty-Anne Rhodes

ISBN: 978-1-291-37970-9
Originally published April 2013

Her vignettes explode and when they are done, our familiar furniture is not in the same place. For that matter, neither are we.   *Tim Page*

Hard captures a fascinating series of tiny truths about the lost people, the quirky, the wanderers of the European world.   *JP Reese*

Glass Animals
by Stephen V. Ramey

ISBN: 978-1-300-66220-4
Originally published January 2013

Equally irreverent and real, these forty-five flash and micro-sized tales left me feeling as though I'd spent time inside the heads of forty-five different people.   *H.G. Estok*

Ramey takes on the richness of his characters' emotional and physical torment and delivers something morbidly fascinating and keen. A great first collection.   *Kristine Ong Muslim*

Each story is the equivalent of looking at the world through a kaleidoscope and the shattered, glittering stories that make up this collection are exceptional.   *James Claffey*

Wild: a collection
by Gill Hoffs

ISBN: 978-1-4717-4215-6
Originally published June 2012

From mermaids to moors and basements to beaches ... Gill Hoffs takes us on a wild ride through the Yorkshire wilderness to Victorian England, the coasts of Japan, Scotland and Ireland, and a 1920s American train, in this collection of fact, fiction and the half-truths in between.

Gill Hoffs' writing, fiction and non, swells with the power of life, sometimes life at the expense of other lives, but always animated and alive.   *Ronnie Scott*

Vestal Aversion
by Matt Potter

ISBN: 978-1-4717-1397-2
Originally published May 2012

A month of stories ... desperate divas, ambitious execs, cuckolded housewives, puzzled politicians and nasty neighbours ... people funny ... and unfunny too.

His range is wide, exploring topics from extramarital affairs to mean-spirited childhood pranks, and his characters always come through as very human ... entertaining and often thought-provoking.   *Richard Bon*

For the complete range of *Pure Slush*
books and eBooks, visit the *Pure Slush Store* at
http://pureslush.webs.com/store.htm